# A Winding Path

Miriam's Journal

_Carrie Bender_

# A Winding Path

HERALD PRESS
Scottdale, Pennsylvania
Waterloo, Ontario

**Library of Congress Cataloging-in-Publication Data**
Bender, Carrie
    A winding path / Carrie Bender.
        p. cm.
    "Miriam's journal 2."
    Sequel to: A fruitful vine.
    ISBN 0-8361-3656-X
    1. Family—Pennsylvania—Fiction.  2. Amish—Pennsylvania—
Fiction.  I. Title.
PS3552. E53845W5  1994
813'.54—dc20                                          93-44864
                                                        CIP

The paper used in this publication is recycled and meets the minimum
requirements of American National Standard for Information
Sciences—Permanence of Paper for Printed Library Materials, ANSI
Z39.48-1984.

Scripture quotations and allusions imbedded in the text are based on
the *King James Version of the Holy Bible*, with some adaptation to
current English usage. For a list of references, see the back of the book.

A WINDING PATH
Copyright © 1994 by Herald Press, Scottdale, Pa. 15683
    Published simultaneously in Canada by Herald Press,
    Waterloo, Ont. N2L 6H7. All rights reserved
Library of Congress Catalog Number: 93-44864
International Standard Book Number: 0-8361-3656-X
Printed in the United States of America
Book design by Paula M. Johnson
Cover art and illustrations by Joy Dunn Keenan
Series logo by Merrill R. Miller

03 02 01 00 99 98 97 96 95 94  10 9 8 7 6 5 4 3 2
12,500 copies in print

*To Rachel and
Rebecca, my favorite
encouragers*

# Contents

# *Hospitality*

*October 16*

*T*oday when husband Nate came home from town, he had a surprise for me. I went out to help unhitch the horse. He smilingly hid something behind his back and asked, "Which hand do you want?"

As usual, I chose the wrong hand, but he gave it to me anyway. A brand-new journal with shiny leather covers! Crisp, clean white pages, waiting to be filled.

My fingers were itching to start writing, but I had to wait. First I helped Nate unhitch the horse and carriage, got two-and-a-half-year-old Dora interested in playing with her toy shovel and bucket in the sandbox, and rocked both babies, Amanda and Peter, to sleep.

I've been wanting to buy another diary all summer. But we were so busy that trips to town were few and far between, and somehow I never got one until now.

Meanwhile, I missed not being able to jot down my thoughts and feelings and to write about our twin babies. They've passed the half-year mark and are at a cute and lovable age. Peter now weighs eighteen pounds, is healthy and robust, and every day looks more like a miniature version of Nate—red hair, ruddy complexion, and the same tilt to the nose.

Sweet, dark-haired little Amanda has a hard time keeping up with Peter. She tilts the scales at barely fifteen pounds. But the doctor says she's doing well despite the fact that she has glutaric aciduria and must be on a low protein diet. Now if we can only keep her glutaric acid levels from going too high! We'll do our part, but it's all in God's hands, "and we know that all things work together for good to them that love God."

The trees along the creek are a riot of color just now. Splashes of vivid reds, browns, and golds are trying to overpower the green and vying with each other for the showiest display. It's a time of year I love. Most of the cornfields have been cut already, with only a few acres left for husking. Now the countryside looks so spacious.

I wish I could go for a brisk walk over the corn-stubble fields and back, under the blue, blue autumn sky, breathing in the crisp, invigorating air with a tang of frost in it. But I can't. I'm tied down to the care of the house and the babies, yet I love every minute of it.

I thank God daily for my children, my health, my work, and my dear husband, Nate. Sometimes I have to think, "All this and heaven too"? (Matthew Henry). ✖

*October 24*

*N*iece Barbara babysat for me this afternoon, and I spent a glorious two hours helping Nate husk corn. I drank deeply of the sights and sounds and smells of the great outdoors and stored it away in my memory for days when I'm cooped up inside: the bright orange of the pile of pumpkins at the edge of the field, the yellow, lavender, and wine-red chrysanthemums, the ripe autumn sunshine, the pungent earth smells.

Nate laughed at my delight in the whole scene and declared, "We'll have to do this oftener."

The part I liked best, though, was the uninterrupted time to have a real heart-to-heart talk with him once again. There are still some things about him that I don't know. Most married couples in their forties have already spent at least twenty years together. Yet Nate and I have only been married less than one and a half years.

This afternoon he told me of some things that happened during his *rumschpringe* (running-around) years. He and his buddies used to play a lot of good-natured pranks on each other at the young people's singings. Some of them were really funny and maybe sometime I'll write them down.

It was a satisfying feeling, too, to see the wagon filling up with golden ears of corn. The workhorses start and stop at Nate's command even without the use of the reins. His faithful old collie dog died a few weeks ago, and now we're thinking of getting a puppy, but haven't yet decided what kind.

We need a farm dog, one that's able to herd the cows and be a good watchdog. Yet we want it to be gentle and playful with the children, too.

Both babies just woke up and are trying to outdo each other in calling for attention, so I'd better go. ✖

*October 30*

*I* got a very disturbing letter in the mail today. Maybe I shouldn't feel that way—I should be glad for the privilege of doing something for someone else and sharing my blessings. It was from Priscilla. She wonders if she could come and live with us.

She would like to be near Dora and watch her grow up. Priscilla is glad Dora has the privilege of growing up in a family with a mother and dad, and yet she would like to have a share in her life, too.

Well, I really can't blame her. After all, she is Dora's mother.

Nate says, "It's up to you. You'll have to make the decision."

I'm praying about it and wanting to give up my own will in the matter, but it's hard to do. We're so happy here together, alone, as a family. I'm afraid her coming would somehow spoil our happiness. And I want Dora as my own daughter.

Would Priscilla insist that Dora call her "Mamma" then, instead of me? Would I be able to bear that?

My eyes followed Dora all the rest of the day as she went about her play, and there was a lump in my throat and tears were near the surface. Her dainty heart-shaped face, velvety dusky eyes, dear little ways.

Dora talks in sentences now and is becoming a real little mother's helper. She's good with the twins, too. There is a fear in my heart that Priscilla would eventually want to take Dora away from us.

Somewhere, out in the world, Dora has a dad, too. What if he would come back to claim both his wife, Priscilla, and daughter Dora?

I can't help but think that it is Priscilla's own fault that she is in this mess. She brought her own troubles upon her head by running off and marrying a divorced man. But I don't want to be hard-hearted and unforgiving.

O God, help me to make the right decision. She has repented and come back to the church, and you have accepted her. Can I do any less? ✖

*T*his forenoon at church, I sat listening to Isaac expounding the Scriptures in his clear, straightforward, earnest way. My thoughts traveled back to just over one year ago when he was ordained preacher by lot, then back to four years ago when he was a young widower and I was working for him and little Matthew.

Isaac was dating Priscilla then, and he was heartbroken when she ran off to marry a divorced man. We all rejoiced when Isaac began dating Rosemary. She sure makes a good preacher's wife, gracious and wholesome. Little Rosabeth is now two years old, and Rosemary is again glowing with the beauty of reaffirmed motherhood, expecting another baby.

During the noon fellowship meal, Rosabeth slipped away from Rosemary and ran to Isaac and threw her arms around his legs, crying *"Daed! Daed!"*

In her expectant condition, Rosemary was embarrassed to rescue her, so Preacher Dan's wife went for her.

Rosabeth clung to Isaac's legs and cried, *"Nee, ich welle bei Daed bleiwe* (no, I want to stay with Daddy)." But she finally consented to be led back to her mother. The brothers and sisters of the congregation exchanged a few smiles.

Now it is afternoon. Dora is taking her nap, and Nate is on the floor playing with the babies. Peter is crawling and romping all over him, and Amanda sits placidly beside him, exploring his hair and face.

My dear little family! How I treasure each moment with them.

Last week I again felt the first faint stirrings of life within, something that never ceases to thrill me. I have to admit, though, that when I had first found out, my reaction was, *Oh no, not so soon again! How will I ever manage to get my work done?*

However, I'm certainly happy about it. Perhaps having Priscilla here to help me will be the answer. When I wrote to her and told her that she's welcome to come and live with us, she sent a letter by return mail. She's coming next week!

Priscilla claimed that she's in better health than she ever was before. She feels certain that her blood disorder will never return and that she is completely healed.

These words have a familiar ring to them, and I wonder if she is right. For her sake, I hope so. ✖

*November 17*

*W*inter came early this year. The leaves are dropping thick and fast, driven before a chilly wind. Monday was a lovely, golden Indian summer day, though, and Nate watched the babies while Dora and I walked along the creek gathering shellbarks and hickory nuts.

We saw flocks of wild geese winging their way south-ward and frisky squirrels busily gathering nuts for the win-ter. Black-capped chickadees, flocks of tiny snowbirds, and agile nuthatches flitted among the trees and up and down the trunks.

We even had the courage to cross the high *Kette-Schtecke* (swinging bridge) to the other side of the creek. I thought Dora might be afraid to cross, but she loved it, and I made sure to hold her hand all the way.

Then on Tuesday, Priscilla arrived with her belongings. She's looking quite well and seems to be in excellent health, energetic, and in good spirits. She helped finish the housecleaning with a right good will, then started raking leaves in the yard.

Dora seems to like her and wants to be with her whenever she can. So far Priscilla hasn't asked for Dora to call her "Mama," and I'm glad for that.

Tuesday evening when we were lingering around the supper table, Priscilla went to her room and brought down a newspaper clipping. It was a July account with a picture of a man who was killed in a motorcycle accident.

"That was my husband," she said quietly, showing no emotion. "You remember, he left me after we had been married only four months—just like he left his first wife. And all the time I was sick in the hospital, he never showed up once."

I stared at her for a long moment before her news really sank in.

Nate voiced the words on the tip of my tongue. "That means you're . . . a—a . . . free. . . ." He stopped, letting the words hang in midair.

Priscilla nodded. "It's tragic that he died that way, but this takes a burden off my shoulders. I feel like God is erasing the sins of my past and giving me a fresh start. I feel so lighthearted."

She brushed away a few tears. By the light of the gasoline lamp, I suddenly noticed how young and pretty Priscilla really was. Would some Amish young man become interested in her sometime? But what about her other problems—that she had needed counseling for?

Priscilla was still talking. "I'm so glad I gave Dora my own last name. I didn't know at first that it would be legal, but when I found it out, I changed it to Kauffman. I've often wished I'd have kept my own last name myself, too. Sometimes I feel like going to the bother of having it changed, even now."

She stroked a few stray gray hairs underneath her prayer covering and sighed.

*It would change if you would marry again,* I thought, but of course I didn't say it out loud. I merely told her, "Yes, and then I'm glad you let us adopt Dora and give her the Mast name. It helps her fit into the family better."

Suddenly I remembered that it's not certain we'll be able to keep Dora. Fear pierced my heart again.

O God, please keep your protecting hand over Dora all the days of her life. May your will be done.

*November 21*

Today Nate and I were at beloved Grandma's funeral (the mother of Frieda, Allen's first wife). Finally her poor heart gave out.

I'll always be thankful that God spared her for that time I was working for Allen while he was a widower and missing Frieda so much. The children needed their mother so badly, too.

Grandma was a blessing to us all, and I learned some deep spiritual truths from her. Seeing her worn and lined face there in her coffin brought tears to my eyes, but I reminded myself of how happy she now must be. For a long while, she had already been homesick for heaven. Grandma was one of God's dear saints, if there ever was one. "Precious in the sight of the Lord is the death of his saints."

Seeing Allen and Polly and the family there together brought the memories crowding back. At first when I was working for Allen, I didn't quite feel "at home" there, but later I grew attached to them all and knew it would be hard to give them up when I had to leave.

Allen couldn't have chosen a better wife and mother for the children. Polly is still the same warm, caring, lovable person that she always was. As she clasped my hand and greeted me with a holy kiss, I felt that it was genuine friendship and not just a duty. Little Mary ran to me and hugged me, and Rachel shyly greeted me, too.

As we drove home through the deepening twilight, old Sorrel's hooves beating on the pavement, and the first snowflakes of the season floating idly down through the stark bare trees, I was absorbed in thought. My life had been lonely and narrow since I was an only child and then was caring for aged parents. I thought of the roundabout way I had come to where I am today.

What if Nate had never spied me trespassing in his meadow? What if I had never been in an accident and broken my leg? When we are living in the center of God's will, is every minute and detail of our lives planned by God?

As if reading my mind, Nate impulsively reached over, clasped my hand in his, and half shyly asked me, "Are you glad you married me, or do you wish you'd have married Allen?"

"I'm so glad I married you," I told him, snuggling close to him and meaning it with all my heart.

He tucked the carriage robe around me, and it seemed almost like we were dating again—just the two of us. This was the first time in a long while that we had gone away together without the babies, and it made me feel young and romantic.

My heartstrings were also tugged homeward, and as we drove in the lane, I spied three little faces at the window. Dora was waving to us. It was a warm, cheery welcome, the babies crowding around me happily, and a wonderful aroma coming from the kitchen.

Already I'm wondering how we managed without Priscilla. She had a fire crackling in the grate, a kettle of mush bubbling merrily on the stove, and apple crisp baking in the oven. Dora ran to me, threw her arms around me, and cried, "Mama!"

I don't know who was gladder to see me, she or the babies. They both wiggled all over with delight and held out their arms to be picked up.

Thank you, God, for my precious family. May I never take any of them for granted. ✖

*November 27*

*A*pple butter cooking time! We don't make as much as some people do, but it's a day-long job. *Schnitzing, schnitzing,* and more *schnitzing* (cutting) of apples. Then filling the big copper furnace kettle with the chopped apples and having someone constantly stirring them with the big wooden stirrer. No wonder the Dutch word for apple butter is *Lattwarick,* which means "a lot of work."

Yet just the aroma of the cooking apples is worth it. Neighbors "Drafty" Dave and Annie came to help, and we'll share the finished product with them.

I can sure understand how that couple got their nickname. He's a real windbag, and she's not far behind. But our people don't give nicknames to be nasty. It's just that so many go by the same name that they almost have to invent extra handles for identification.

I don't know how Annie always manages to be the first to find out the news of this district, but somehow, she does. As soon as she came in the door, she proudly announced that early this morning a bouncing little dishwasher joined Isaac and Rosemary's family, and they named her Anna Ruth. I'm so happy for them, that the birth is over and all is well.

Drafty Dave is a born storyteller, and in his nearly seventy years he has accumulated a wealth of tales. He sure kept things from getting monotonous. Whenever he paused for breath while telling a story, Annie squeezed in a little neighborhood gossip edgewise.

However, she's not malicious; neither of them are. They're both good-souled and kindhearted, and I doubt that they have a single enemy. Everybody loves them, I'm sure.

Oh yes! The biggest news of all is that Dave's have taken in a boarder, a young man named Henry Crawford. He hails from Georgia and is very interested in the Amish way of life. He'd like to live among the Amish for a while and possibly later join the church. Time will tell, whether or not he's sincere.

He'd like to get to know the neighbors, so we invited Dave's to bring him here for supper on Saturday evening. I'll have to see to it that we have freshly baked bread to go with the apple butter. We'll give him a taste of Pennsylvania Dutch cooking and old-fashioned hospitality. ✖

*December 2*

*T*oday was our no-church Sunday, so we spent a quiet day at home. We awoke to a dazzlingly beautiful world this morning—every bush, branch, and twig was covered with hoarfrost. It was a real winter wonderland.

Dora ran to the window and cried, "Mama, look, everything is *wunderbaar schee!* (wonderful nice)."

It's not often that we have such a display so early in the season.

Drafty Dave's brought Henry Crawford for supper last evening, as we had planned. He has black hair, a black moustache, and dark almost piercing eyes. Henry is tall and slender and acts like a real gentleman.

There's only one thing about his mannerisms that bothers me. He never looks others straight in the eye, almost as if he didn't want to meet an honest gaze. Oh well, maybe I'm just being judgmental.

Henry's extreme politeness was somewhat disconcerting, too. As we passed the dishes around the table, every time a dish was passed to him, he said, "Thank you, ma'am."

After a while, though, I got used to his "yes, please, pardon, excuse me, thank you, Ma'am. . . ." We plain people are not used to so much of that. We try to be kind and obey the golden rule, though, and do say "thank you" if someone gives a gift or does a favor for us, and "I'm sorry" when we hurt or offend someone.

I noticed Henry covertly watching Priscilla all evening, seeming to be fascinated, while Dave entertained us with his stories. Because of the visitor, we had to speak English so he could understand.

Sometimes the funniest part of all was Drafty Dave's "Dutchified" English. Several times I noticed Nate trying hard to keep from laughing when Dave put in a Dutch (Pennsylvania *Deutsch,* German) word by mistake.

Henry, however, didn't seem to be bothered in the least with Dave's "chust" for "just," and "wisit" for "visit," and other such phrases peppered throughout his stories. Henry was too busy watching Priscilla.

While we women did the dishes, Annie told us that Henry had sold his car and was looking for a horse and carriage. He really must be serious about trying out the Amish way of life. Come spring, he wants to work for an Amish farmer, too.

When they left, Henry complimented Priscilla and me on the good meal. He thanked us profusely, although he had eyes only for Priscilla. To her, he commented, "I hope to see you again very soon."

Well! I just hope he's sincere. ✄

*N*o snow for Christmas. Somehow it doesn't seem like Christmas with no snow on the ground. But I'm fastening my thoughts on the real meaning of the day, the reason for rejoicing: the gift of God's own Son to this lost world. What an "unspeakable gift," the gift of the hope of salvation. "Joy to the world!"

We went to see little Anna Ruth at Isaac's. She looks like her dad, there's no doubt about it. She's really a cute little thing.

Priscilla opted to stay home, and when we got back, she was gone. I thought perhaps she had left for a walk along the creek. But when it was nearly dark, an unfamiliar horse and buggy came driving in the lane, and Priscilla hopped off. I couldn't make out who the driver was, but when Priscilla came in, all smiles, she informed us it was none other than Henry Crawford.

"He shaved off his moustache and wants to grow a beard," she chuckled. "And he handles his horse like an old pro. We'll make an Amishman out of him yet."

"However did you happen to go out with him?" I asked curiously. I wondered if Priscilla had gotten lonely and had gone looking for company.

"Oh, we hadn't planned it. I was just out for a walk, and he came driving by."

She flashed a coquettish smile, and for an instant I wondered if Priscilla was back to her old tricks of flirting, but then I quickly dismissed that idea.

"He's really very interesting," she went on in a lively tone. "You can tell he's an educated man. He's smart, and he knows a lot. He asked if he might have the pleasure of driving me to church on Sunday, and I told him I'd like that, but it would not be the proper thing to do. Maybe someday, though."

She winked at me and laughingly went upstairs to her room.

It made me feel faintly uneasy to see her acting so enthusiastic about Henry so quickly. We know so little about him. What if he would do like a few other outsiders who come to the Amish church? Some seem so sincere, but then after a year or two, they leave it all and go back out into the world.

On the other hand, my thoughts turned to the ones who had remained faithful. One had come over to the Amish from the Catholic Church, married an Amish girl, and now they were raising a large family. He seemed as dependable and stalwart in the faith as any born Amishman.

That evening I pondered the problems Priscilla has had in the past. Is it my duty to nip this thing in the bud before it really gets started? Or is it God's will? I feel like I've meddled in other people's affairs too often.

O heavenly Father, help us all! I don't want to see anyone get hurt again. I will cast all my cares upon you. Lead us and guide us, and help us to make the right decisions. ✖

*December 29*

*T*oday was a warm and balmy day, more like Indian summer than winter. Priscilla and I took the babies outside to get some sunshine, and Dora frolicked happily around us.

These days Peter takes a few steps alone, walking along the furniture and holding onto it. Amanda hasn't progressed that far yet, but no one is trying to rush her. We'll let her develop at her own pace.

I will accept all my children exactly as they are and try not to make them over into something they weren't meant to be. Always I want to give them the priceless gift of unconditional love, the kind of love that God has for his children, though weak and prone to sin.

We put the twins in the baby coach and wheeled them into the barn to see the animals. A barn is such a friendly place, warm and inviting, and full of animal smells. Dora loves being in it. Soon she had her arms full of friendly, purring kittens.

The horses nickered a friendly greeting, too, and the

cows watched us with solemn eyes while chewing their cud. Pigeons cooed from the rafters, and a few banties scratched in the feed aisle. The children liked the squealing piggies best of all and were reluctant to leave.

When we stepped out into the bright sunshine, I spied a familiar figure trudging up the lane. Rosemary! And her baby's only a month old! She was smiling, but her face seemed to lack the usual radiance.

Priscilla offered to put the children to bed for their naps. She took them upstairs, while Rosemary and I sat at the kitchen table, visiting.

At first we talked of nothing but the weather: "How unseasonably warm it still is," "Will we have a big blizzard this winter?" and so forth. Yet I got the impression that here was a "damsel in distress."

I poured two cups of fresh-brewed meadow tea and laid out sugar cookies, all the time wondering what the trouble was.

"Ah, this hits the spot," Rosemary exclaimed as she sipped the tea. "I get so thirsty when I have a nursing baby. Which reminds me, I can't stay long. Sister Ruth is with the baby, and she'll be hungry again before too long.

"I just had to have a talk with you, Miriam," she went on, swallowing hard. "I wanted to visit with you alone when you were at our place on Christmas Day, but I didn't have the chance since there was a roomful of other company."

Rosemary absentmindedly traced a pattern on the tablecloth with her spoon. "It's Isaac," she murmured, finally. "He—uh—well . . . did you hear about the new settlement they're starting in Minnesota?"

I nodded.

"He says he feels it's God's will for us to move there,

too." She barely whispered the words.

"Move to Minnesota?" I echoed, blankly. "Why?"

She shrugged her shoulders. "Oh, Miriam, how can I tell him I don't want to go when he feels sure it's God's will? I love him, but how can I leave my parents, brothers and sisters, and friends to go to a faraway state where I don't know anyone?" She covered her face with her hands.

I tried to think of something to say to Rosemary, to comfort her. Finally I made a stab at it. "I can see why you are so upset, Rosemary. That would be a big move. We would miss you, too! How can I give you up?"

Rosemary gave me a look of appreciation, knowing I also would feel the pains of parting.

Yet I thought I had to help her put things into perspective. "At least you wouldn't be traveling in a covered wagon, or going into hostile territory like the pioneers had to do. They often didn't hear from their loved ones back home again for years, and sometimes they never saw them again.

"Anyhow, we could write letters to each other. And occasionally we could even hire a van or take the train and visit back and forth."

"That's so," Rosemary agreed. "Maybe I'm acting childish. I'll get over this after a while."

I reached over and touched her hand tenderly. "Just remember, we're your friends for always, even if you are in Minnesota."

She smiled wanly, brushed the crumbs from her apron, and got up briskly. "I just must get back to my baby. Thanks for listening to me. Maybe it will never come to pass, anyway. Isaac was ordained for this district, and it would have to go through the counsel of the church. Maybe the move would be discouraged."

"Didn't Isaac ask how you felt about it at all?" I asked.

"No, he didn't. I suppose he assumed I'd be as enthusiastic as he is. I believe he's taking this as an opportunity to 'go into all the world and preach the gospel to every creature.' Perhaps he has hopes that the Amish community in Minnesota will show all the neighbors what it means to really be disciples of Jesus."

I glanced quickly at Rosemary, but there was not a trace of sarcasm in her face.

"Well," I groped for some way to encourage Rosemary, "God will not require something of you that's too hard for you. When you are in the center of God's will, he will hold you 'in the hollow of his hand,' and comfort, strengthen, and keep you."

"Thanks, Miriam. I needed that," Rosemary said quietly. "I feel a lot better."

When I told Nate about it tonight, he blew out a long, low whistle. "I wonder if Isaac perhaps doesn't have more zeal than sense. He was ordained for here.

"Minnesota yet! Doesn't it get a lot colder there? By the way, the wind is rising right here and the temperature is dropping fast. It's already gone down at least twenty degrees. I heard the windmill clanging and whining in the gale, and I had to shiver."

As I dropped a big chunk of wood on the fire, I thought, *Right now, I'm glad I don't have a zealous husband.* ✖

# *Partings*

*W*e had church at our house today, and I'm so glad it's over. Although I am almost slender compared to how I looked one year ago, I still felt self-conscious about my appearance. I almost wished it would still be like it was a generation ago. As soon as a woman "showed," she stayed at home and did not even attend church services. At least I'm fairly certain there will be only one baby this time.

We had lots of help all week, and with Priscilla here to help care for the children, getting ready for church was a breeze.

The news has leaked out that Isaac is interested in moving to Minnesota, and tongues sure have been wagging.

Rosemary is her gracious self again, serene and unperturbed. If anyone shows *Gelassenheit* (being yielded to the Lord), she is surely one of them.

Priscilla hovered behind Henry when the men were seated at the dinner table. She made sure that he had plenty of rolls and spreads, smearcase, red beets, tea, and *Schnitzboi* (apple pie).

I couldn't help but worry about Priscilla last week when she went out with Henry two evenings in a row. Finally I mustered up the courage to have a long talk with her.

She heartily assured me that she's "going very slowly." She says she's not letting her heart run away with her, and that Henry will have to prove himself before she will fully trust him.

Priscilla also assured me that her old feelings are gone. She has forgiven her dad. The counseling helped her get rid of the resentment and bitterness inside. If she ever gets married again, it will be for love and not for spite.

"But you must realize," I cautioned, "that Henry is a young man of, what is it, twenty-eight years? He's never been married. He likely would have done his share of running around."

With that, Priscilla stamped her foot and her eyes flashed fire. "So that's what you're thinking of! But I could say the same thing about Nate. He was a lot older than Henry when he got married! How do you like that!"

"But Nate was a Christian, and Henry was a man of the world, remember?" I said gently.

A few of the neighbors arrived then, to help get ready for church, and the conversation was interrupted, but I wished I hadn't said anything. I hadn't realized Priscilla was so sensitive about it, or I would've bitten my tongue before I spoke.

Later that evening Priscilla came and apologized to me for her outburst.

I assured her, "It was my fault, and in the future I'll try to mind my own business better."

"No, you were probably right," she conceded. "But remember, I was no angel either. If he's willing to overlook my past, I'll do the same for him."

"None of us are angels," I reminded her. "And if he has

accepted Christ, as he claims he has, and is trying to live for God, I see no reason why you shouldn't forgive his past, whatever it may have been."

She smiled a tremulous smile, and we were friends again. ✖

*January 11*

*B*rrrr! A genuine, old-fashioned blizzard is raging outside. The wind keeps drifting the fluffy, white stuff higher and higher! Oh well, let it snow *now* rather than early March, when we'll be needing to go to the hospital—that is, if I won't be able to persuade the doctor to consent to a home delivery this time.

The trees along the creek are a glorious sight, and the creek itself looks like a white, icy, frozen waterway. Nate has been wading through the drifts to the barn and back, battling frozen water pipes. I'm keeping kettles of boiling water on the range constantly and feeling mighty thankful for the mountain of wood Nate chopped last fall and stacked into the wood shanty.

Peter and Amanda are in their high chairs eating their breakfast, and I'm trying to teach them to eat with a spoon. Amanda is getting the hang of it nicely, but Peter's slopping more on the floor and in his hair than into his mouth. Priscilla sits there laughing at him while knitting a vest for Henry, and Dora's at the window watching the snow.

On Wednesday afternoon Drafty Dave and Annie made a call here. Since Priscilla had already invited Henry for supper (she's giving him lessons in speaking Dutch), we invited them to stay, too.

Priscilla had made *Schnitz un Gnepp* (apples and dumplings), but Henry politely declined to taste it, much to her disappointment. Dave and Annie did justice to it, though, and raved about how delicious it was. Henry will have to get used to some of these Pennsylvania Dutch dishes. He really liked the oyster stew, though.

Dave was telling about his trip to town last week and airing some of his pet peeves. "Every time we go to town, there's a new building going up somewhere. The streets just keep getting closer to us. It sure is a pity to see all that good farmland going for development.

"Maybe we should all be minded like Isaac, to move to Minnesota, where there's more room and less people. So much traffic here! Ei yi yi!

"At the store there was such a long line at the checkout counter. Then just when it was my turn to pay, the computer or cash register busted yet and wouldn't work anymore.

"The young snip of a clerk had to figure out the change by hand. She stood there counting her fingers and just couldn't decide how much she owed me. Finally she said, 'Sir, can you tell me what change I owe you?' Imagine that!"

Dave snorted, then started off on his next gripe. "They say nowadays that these high school kids aren't even learning to read and figure! They have calculators and computers and watch movies all the time, but they don't learn the three basic R's—readin', 'ritin', and 'rithmetic." He shook his head in disgust.

"Now Dave," Annie protested gently. "We have nothing to complain about."

"I don't believe it's all that bad," Priscilla protested,

glancing at Henry. "Tell him he's exaggerating. You would know."

Henry merely shrugged his shoulders and said, "I don't know much about the younger generation. All I know is that *I* learned to read and figure." He went on eating his salad, his face expressionless.

Annie commented, "We should just be thankful that we're allowed to have our own schools where our children are not influenced by newfangled inventions and worldly ways. Yet they still learn plenty, just what they need to live our way."

This kicked off a lively discussion about Amish parochial schools versus public schools. Priscilla insisted that public schools are better in one way, that children learn more there, but Dave heartily disagreed.

Finally Henry spoke up. "You people stick to your private schools. You wouldn't believe some of the things going on behind the teachers' backs where I went to school. I even had drugs offered to me in grade school already, and it's probably worse nowadays."

Changing the subject, Henry asked, "Did you hear about the things that got stolen on Sunday while we were having services here?"

When he saw the blank looks on our faces, he went on. "Some of the carriages were in back of the barn. Those closest to the road—someone stole the buggy robes and carriage blankets out of them. Most people didn't notice until they had started for home. One of the neighbors told me about it this afternoon."

I noticed a look of utter amazement on Annie's face. For once she wasn't the first to have found out about something.

"Well, I declare," she exclaimed. "What's this world coming to?" She shook her head sadly, clucking her tongue.

That was pretty much the reaction of us all. It gives me the shivers to think that we have robbers in the neighborhood. Next it won't be safe to go outside after dark, like in the cities.

Oh well, as long as we're snowed in like this, I guess we won't have to worry about thieves. If they are so determined not to work for a living, they would hardly care to struggle through this storm.

Time to go wash the babies' faces and hands, and almost everything else. ✖

*January 21*

*G*loria Graham came to the house tonight and wondered whether we'd be willing to keep her white Persian cat for a fortnight while she goes on a trip. She's one of our neighbors and a regular milk customer.

I was ready to say, *Sure, that shouldn't be a problem.* But then as she kept talking, I gathered that Kitty Kat is a spoiled, pampered, petted house cat. She would expect us to keep her in the house while she's here.

I changed my mind and said, "Well, you know, I have two babies crawling all over the floor. I wouldn't want them constantly picking up cat hair."

"Oh no, no," Gloria protested. "Kitty Kat is the cleanest cat I ever saw. She simply doesn't shed hair. I'll bring her litter box and little padded bed. She sleeps most of the day.

Let me bring her in right now, and you can see for yourself how adorable she is."

Gloria went to the car and brought in the most gorgeous, fluffy white cat I ever saw. A big pink ribbon was attached to her collar, and she blinked pale green eyes benevolently at us.

Dora stared at her in wide-eyed awe and took a few steps backward, but Peter scooted across the floor, making a beeline for the cat.

"You may stroke her fur," Gloria said indulgently to Dora. "Come here. Don't be afraid of her. Kitty Kat never scratches."

Peter got there first, and I held my breath, fearing he would pull her tail or hurt her in some other way. But he only patted her gently, talking softly to her in baby language. Dora finally got the courage to stroke her, and Amanda came crawling to them, too.

"If you folks would be kind enough to let her stay with you," Gloria continued, "I'll gladly pay you whatever you ask, even if it's $10 a day. Let me tell you, Kitty Kat is like a daughter to me. She's the daughter I never had. In fact, she's *all* I have."

She picked up the cat and crooned softly to her, kissing her on the nose. My warning hackles rose, and I sensed that my answer should be no. But just then Priscilla spoke up, "Oh, what an adorable cat! I'm so fond of cats. Please let her stay with us."

Nate was still choring in the barn, and with Priscilla pressuring me, I finally gave my reluctant consent. Gloria is bringing the cat on Friday, along with all her toys and gadgets and beds and boxes—and food, of course.

Oh dear, what have I gotten myself into? ✜

 $W$ ell, our magnificent boarder arrived tonight and is fast asleep in her elaborate kitty bed. She's really a docile cat and no trouble at all. Gloria spent nearly an hour saying good-bye to her beloved Kitty Kat, but she finally left now after putting her to bed. Priscilla and the children are in bed, too, and Nate is still out in the barn with some farrowing sows.

So all is quiet in the kitchen—so quiet that a bold little mouse came out from under the refrigerator and is looking for crumbs under the table. Maybe with a cat in the house for two weeks, we'll be able to get him. He's too smart for my traps.

Henry brought Priscilla home at 9:00 this evening, and she came in starry-eyed and happy and wanting to talk.

"We had a lovely time!" she chattered delightedly. "Henry took me to a restaurant in town, and we had a scrumptious meal. He's so polite and courteous."

She flopped down on the settee and kicked off her shoes.

"Restaurant?" I echoed. "Doesn't he know that plain people usually don't eat in restaurants unless they're traveling a far distance and it's really necessary?"

"Oh, stop being a killjoy!" Priscilla shot back. "There's nothing wrong with eating in a restaurant every now and then, and you know it. Besides, we don't plan to make a habit of it.

"It was ever so much fun. You wouldn't believe how thoughtful Henry is. He never walks ahead of me, he holds doors for me, and he helps me with putting on my bonnet and shawl." She threw back her head and laughed heartily.

"It's really funny sometimes, but I love it.

"Know what he told me tonight?" she went on enthusiastically. "He's planning to make application to join our church this spring, when the young folks do. After he has gone through the instructions and the eighteen articles of faith, and when he is a baptized member of the church, then I'll really know that he's sincere."

After she had gone upstairs, I sat for a long time, deep in thought about Priscilla and Henry and about our own family. Perhaps we do need some new blood in our Amish family lines.

Amanda's glutaric aciduria disease is caused by a defective gene passed down by our ancestors. After several generations of intermarrying (second, third, and fourth cousins), the defective genes have spread throughout our population and tend to become dominant. Now they tell me that, according to the specialist's estimate, one Amish person in seven carries the gene.

Since we marry only among ourselves (marriage outside the faith is forbidden), that ratio isn't likely to get better. The only way it could be improved is by enlarging the gene pool, through childless Amish couples adopting babies and raising them as Amish, or outsiders like Henry joining the Amish and raising families.

Oh, I'm afraid that things won't work out and that someone will get hurt. The words, "Why did you doubt, O you of little faith," keep revolving in my mind. It's true that I am doubting. I don't have much faith in Henry Crawford. I really don't trust him very far.

O heavenly Father, you know and control all things. I don't have to carry this burden myself, when you have told us to cast all our cares upon you. I must keep reminding myself of your promise over and over, that you care for us. Priscilla is your child, and we know that all things work together for good to them that love you. ✖

*O*h, what will we do? How could such a thing have happened? I'm feeling extremely agitated in both body and soul. I'm trying to remind myself, "Why worry when you can pray?" If not even a sparrow can fall without God seeing it, then surely he knows the whereabouts of a stray white Persian cat and can bring her back.

We had a fresh snowfall this morning, then this afternoon it turned mild and sunny. Dora begged to go outside to play in the snow and to make a snowman. I put her boots on, bundled her up warmly, and then went for my own boots and wraps.

Dora must've stood holding open the door as she waited for me. The next minute she was crying, "Mama, *dabber kumm!* (come quick). Kitty Kat ran outside!"

I clumsily dashed outside but saw no cat anywhere. What a desolate feeling! I got Nate to help, and we frantically searched under every shrub and in every tree, everywhere a cat could possibly be hiding.

We tried to follow her tracks in the snow, but with so many footprints of dogs and people around the house, that was hopeless. We were calling, "Here, kitty, kitty, kitty!" It all was to no avail.

I can't imagine what Gloria Graham will say. She plans to be back on the seventh, so that gives us only two more days. I'm "praying without ceasing" that God will somehow bring that cat back, in time. But it's so cold outside again tonight, and I have visions of finding Kitty Kat frozen cold and stiff. She's not used to being outside.

Nate went out to the phone shanty to report the missing cat in the lost-and-found section of the newspaper, but I don't have much hope. ✂

*February* 7

*G*od has let me down. At least that's how I feel. Perhaps my faith wasn't strong enough. The cat has not been found.

Gloria Graham drove in tonight, wrapped in a luxurious-looking fur coat, and her face was wreathed in smiles. "Where's my Kitty Kat?" she sang out, as she opened the door.

Her greeting was met only by silence and dismal stares.

"She's gone," I whispered hoarsely. "She slipped outside when the door was open."

I wish I could draw a curtain across my mind to cover the scene that followed. But I can't blot it from my memory. It's there to haunt me all the time.

Gloria uttered pitiful shrieks and moans, crying for her darling Kitty Kat. She kept saying over and over, "She was all I had, she was all I had."

I cowered miserably in a chair, wishing I'd be anywhere else. After a while her feelings changed to anger, and she threatened to have us sued. Then she left, saying she was going right home to call her lawyer.

I'm afraid sleep is out of the question tonight. Is there

no solution to this my dilemma? I offered to buy her another Persian cat just like Kitty Kat, but she took it as an insult and vehemently refused the offer.

O *Herr, hilf mir* (Lord, help me). What shall we do?

Nate says not to worry, the cat might turn up yet. How can he be so calm? ✖

*I*t's a beautiful world once again, and I'm feeling happy and relieved. This afternoon Nate went to town for supplies, and Henry took Priscilla to visit her mother, so I was alone when the feed-sack man came. He pays for empty feed sacks, so I ransacked the lower barn for all I could find. Then I climbed the steps to the floor above, where we store hay and straw and have the grain in the granary.

Suddenly, out of a dim corner, a big white angel of Persian cat flung herself at me in a frenzy of recognition and genuine delight. She purred and purred, wrapping her entire body around my legs, arching her back to be petted, and meowing happily.

I grabbed her up, and let me tell you, that was the first time I ever kissed a cat! She was as sleek and fat as ever, so she must've dined sumptuously on mice and rats and jumped to the water trough for water. I was determined not to let that cat out of my sight again and held on for dear life when I carried her into the house.

As soon as Nate came home, I sent him posthaste to the phone shanty to call Gloria Graham, and she was here even before Nate came back.

I do believe that cat really is as dear to Gloria as a child would be. Oh my, such a fuss. Such a tearful, joyous fuss over a cat. ✂

*W*hat is love? "Love is an absorbing desire for and delight in another's highest good. Real love is entirely unselfish. It utterly loses sight of self-interest and sets itself to seeking the interest of the person loved."

I copied this out of my devotional book, and I've been lying here thinking about it. These past few weeks I've had plenty of time to read and meditate and pray because I had to lie down and elevate my leg much of the time.

That's the doctor's orders, because of a nasty-looking purple blood clot that developed on my leg. To my disappointment, he told me I won't be able to have a home delivery again this time, as I had hoped.

How thankful I am for Priscilla these days! She is so energetic and cheerful. She makes the work fly and keeps the children happy and contented. I can hear her singing now, above the roar of the gas engine running the washing machine.

Getting back to the verse about love: How easy it is to love the kind and unselfish person, the Spirit-filled Christian.

It says here that the fruit of the Spirit is an affectionate, lovable disposition, a radiant spirit, a cheerful temper, a tranquil mind, a quiet manner, a forbearing patience in provoking circumstances and with trying people, a sympathetic insight and tactful helpfulness, generous judgment, loyalty and reliableness, and under all circumstances humility that forgets self in the joy of others.

Here is also a little verse I learned in school.

When I think of the charming people I know,
　It's surprising how often I find,
The chief of the qualities that make them so,
　Is just that they are kind.

I think this is what makes Nate so charming and why he is so easy to love. He is so kindhearted and unselfish. It fills my heart with gratitude to see how good and tenderhearted he is with the children, too.

Nate's example inspires me with a desire to do my best for him. This reminds me of the words of a wedding song, "There is beauty all around, when there's love at home" (McNaughton).

I'm counting my blessings, shoring myself up for what lies ahead. I guess I must admit that there is some trepidation in my heart, wishing the birth were over, wondering if we'll have another glutaric aciduria baby.

I keep reminding myself of God's promise in Isaiah: "Fear not, for I am with you: be not dismayed; for I am your God: I will strengthen you; . . . yes, I will uphold you with the right hand of my righteousness." ✖

*March 7*

*W*ell, here I am at home again, glad to rest in my own bed, and best of all to have Baby

Sadie there in her little crib, healthy and beautiful. We came home from the hospital at lunchtime and were joyfully welcomed by the little family.

Dora wanted to hold and love "Baby Sister" right away. The babies (oops, I mean the twins! I can't call them babies anymore) wanted to explore the new baby all over with inquisitive little fingers.

In my happiness, my thoughts so often turn to my hospital roommate, Dottie Rogers. She also had a baby girl the same day I did, and we got fairly well acquainted.

Dottie was gloriously happy, but the second day the doctor came in while her husband was there and told them their baby has Down's syndrome.

When the doctor explained the outlook, Dottie just cried and cried. Her husband stood helplessly by, not knowing what to do or say to comfort her.

This is their first baby, and they look like they're in their early or middle twenties. I guess they were simply not prepared for such a possibility.

It's usually the older mothers who have a much greater chance of giving birth to a Down's baby. But apparently it happens to young mothers, too, sometimes.

The doctor tried to say things to lighten their load, to soften the blow, but the tears still flowed. After the doctor left, her husband, Tony, put his arm around her and tried to comfort her, but she pushed him away and cried all the harder. I felt so sorry for them both.

Dottie was sobbing and half choking. After a while, in desperation, her husband turned to me and said, "Mrs. Mast, can't you do something to help her?"

I felt so helpless, not knowing what to say, and quickly racked my brain to think of something. Finally I asked him, "Is she . . . uh . . . are you Christians?"

Tony shook his head. "We just moved here from Virginia last fall, and we've been thinking of starting to go to church, but we haven't gotten around to it yet."

"Do you think maybe you'd better ring for a nurse?" I suggested. "They'd probably give her a sedative."

She slept the rest of the day, then, but the next evening she cried again for several hours.

The young husband finally lost patience with her and told her sharply, "Quit that!"

She did quit for a few seconds, but then her sobs became more uncontrollable than ever.

Tony looked at me and declared, "I can't stand this, I mean it, I'm going home." And he did leave right away.

Eventually Dottie dried her eyes and looked up from her pitiful huddle on the bed. "Where did my husband go?"

"He said he's leaving," I told her. "It was hard for him to see you crying like that when he wasn't able to do or say anything to comfort you."

"Oh, things are going from bad to worse," she moaned. "Tony must be so discouraged."

"I can see that you both are very disappointed," I said softly. "I feel the hurt with you."

"Thank you," she replied. "I don't know how we can handle this. It just seems like such a heavy load."

"Every child is precious," I responded tenderly. "God has chosen you to be the parents of one of his 'Special Children,' as we call them. I understand these children are very sweet and lovable."

"But we were looking forward so much to having a normal, healthy baby," she wailed. "Tony was so happy and excited about it."

"Give yourself time to grieve. Then you and your husband will want to be strong for the sake of your child." I encouraged her and also wanted to give her a goal. "God loves you, and when you find a church, there will be a caring family of God around you."

"Please don't mention God again to me. He could have prevented this, but he didn't. I don't want to know a God like that."

"But he loves you and wants you to be part of his family. Then he will comfort you and carry your burden for you."

"No, no!" She was sobbing again, and a nurse came in to give her some medication.

Since I'm at home, my thoughts are constantly returning to her, and I can't seem to get her off my mind. I want to pray for her, but she doesn't want to be prayed for. ✂

*I*t's so good to be at home again! "Be it ever so humble, there's no place like home" (Payne). This in-between Sunday, with no church service, was a warm time of family togetherness. Anyhow, it was too soon for me to be taking the baby out.

This morning I read in my devotional book, "There is no other place in all the world where the little courtesies of life should be so tenderly given, where living ministrations should be so cheerfully bestowed, such as an offer to help, a careful compliment, a kind caress, in short, where good manners should be so diligently practiced."

Home Sweet Home, the place where childhood days are spent, where habits are formed which are to continue throughout the future. The apostle Paul's counsel can help set the tone for home life: "Be kind one to another, tenderhearted, forgiving one another, even as God for Christ's sake has forgiven you."

Nate thinks Baby Sadie looks just like me, with her head full of dark hair, and he teases me about my little clone. He's even tickled about it. I had been hoping for a red-haired, freckle-faced, cherubic daughter, but what's in the heart will matter so much more.

Last evening, after their Dutch lesson, Priscilla brought Henry in to show him Baby Sadie. She told him to sit in the rocker, then handed the baby to him.

He crooned softly to her, and patted her cheek, then suddenly and unexpectedly, to our surprise and embarrassment, he began to cry. He quickly handed the baby back to Priscilla and went outside.

Priscilla and I stared at each other in consternation. I

had never before seen a man crying.

"What do you think brought that on?" I asked weakly.

She wordlessly shrugged her shoulders and shook her head.

"I know I shouldn't be meddling in your affairs," I said hesitantly, "but I've often wondered, have you told him everything about your past, and that Dora is your daughter?"

"Oh, yes, of course," Priscilla replied quickly. "He said it makes no difference in his love for me."

"Has he offered any information about his past at all?"

"No, he hasn't."

"Maybe you should try to find out a little more."

She shook her head. "It doesn't matter to me. I told you, if he's willing to forgive my past, and loves me all the same, I'm willing to do the same for him."

When Nate was finished choring, the men came back in together. Henry was his usual interesting self.

My heart has somewhat softened toward Henry. Whatever his past has been, somehow I believe he is sincere. But I think Priscilla should try to find out more about his past, and I can't understand why she doesn't want to.

O God, I give to you the reins of my life, and the reins of the lives of my loved ones. We can only see "through a glass, darkly," but you know and understand all things. Lead us and guide us in your will, and let all things work together for good. ✖

*March 13*

*B*aby is doing well, and the visitors we've been having are lavish in exclaiming about her "cuteness." Drafty Dave and Annie asked if they could adopt her and our other children for the grandchildren they never had, since they are childless.

Of course, we are delighted, for we feel our children will miss a lot by not having any living grandparents. Most children have two sets, one on the maternal side, and one on the paternal.

So we agreed together, Dave's and us, to begin calling them Grandma and Grandpa in front of the children. I never liked the nickname Drafty anyway.

Isaac and Rosemary also paid us a visit to see Baby Sadie. They've been so busy packing and getting ready to move, and we haven't been able to help them much at this time. We compared our babies and had a good old-fashioned heart-to-heart talk.

"Wouldn't it be nice if my Anna Ruth and your Sadie could grow up as neighbors and become the best of friends?" Rosemary remarked wistfully.

"It sure would," I responded, just as wistfully. "It sure spites us (makes us sorry) to see you go. But I'm sure you'll make a lot of new friends there. By now, how do you really feel about moving to Minnesota?"

"Oh, I've resigned myself to it," Rosemary said cheerfully. "I'm even getting rather excited. Isaac's enthusiasm is contagious. And I know that if we want to go, it's best to go when the children are small."

"I really have to admire your spunk," I told her. "It takes courageous, talented people like you to help make a go of the new settlement."

"I hope you'll write often," she murmured, clasping my hand. "I'm going to miss you so much."

"I will," I promised her. "It will make you seem closer.

When I'm lonely for you, I'll be thinking that it's the ones left behind who are the losers.

"I've been told that our church doubles every twenty years or so, and there sure isn't enough farmland around here. There's not much of a future in farming here for the children."

"Now you're sounding just like Isaac." Rosemary laughed. "Next thing we'll be hearing that you're planning to join us, too."

Later, when I told Nate about our conversation, he mused, "Maybe if I'd be twenty years younger. . . ." ✖

*March 20*

*T*hese last days I'm feeling much more peppy again, and the blood clot on my leg is completely cleared up and gone. Baby Sadie usually wakes up only once each night, so Nate doesn't have to help at night like he did with the twins.

Around midnight I was up with Baby Sadie and thought I heard a faint noise outside. So I went to the bedroom window and peeped through the curtain, to see if everything was all right outside. Near the barn, I saw a shadow moving, then disappear around the corner of the barn.

A few minutes later I thought I heard a car or truck start up out on the road. I quickly awoke Nate, and he dressed and went outside with the flashlight.

When Nate came back, he was looking grim and said someone had definitely been in the barn. The big double doors were wide open, and one of his prize veal calves was missing.

*Ach* (oh) my! Not thieves on the place again, out here in the peaceful countryside! Is someone targeting us for theft? I hope not. I haven't heard of anyone else in the neighborhood having trouble with thieves. May the thieves soon be caught and justly dealt with. ✄

*March 23*

*I* put all the baby cards we received up on the wall, and it's a nice display. Just today we received one from Polly, Allen, and family. Polly wrote a long, newsy letter—the kind I love to receive. She says she is experiencing "change of life" and having a difficult time of it. I guess I'll have to face that in a year or two.

Mary has learned to write and sent along a sweet little note. It's good to know she hasn't forgotten me yet.

After I read the letters, I sat rocking Baby Sadie, and the memories of working for Allen and his family came crowding back: milking the kicker cow, Rachel's lack of cooperation, and the little boy's mischievousness.

Dora pulled her little rocker beside mine and rocked her baby dolly to sleep, too. My thoughts turned to the day Priscilla brought her baby to me there at Allen's place and asked me to raise her.

Then there was my accident, when I broke my leg and Polly took my place at Allen's and eventually married him. In looking back, I really do believe that all things work together for good to those who love God, even though, in the midst of our struggles, it's hard to believe. "In all your ways acknowledge him, and he shall direct your paths." ✄

*S*pring's here! The willow trees along the creek are showing faint signs of green, and robins seem to be singing everywhere.

The breezes that blow up from the meadow are scented of flowers and fields with freshly plowed earth, and they're calling me to the great outdoors. I have my garden seeds ready, and I can hardly bear to let Priscilla do the planting this year. That's one of my favorite tasks.

Nate went to help Isaac and Rosemary load their truck this morning. Then tomorrow they're off for Minnesota!

While Nate was gone, we had a scare—a driverless horse and buggy came tearing in the lane, bouncing sometimes on only two wheels, barely missing the gatepost, and then stopping at the barn. The horse was breathing heavily, his sides heaving.

"Oh dear!" Priscilla cried. "That looks like Henry's horse." She ran outside, and I followed close behind.

"It *is* Henry's horse," she said in a panicky voice. "Do you think he was thrown off and hurt?"

"Probably not," I replied. "See, the lines are wrapped around the dash. Maybe the horse tore loose somehow, and it certainly knows the way to come in our lane." I began to unhitch the horse to put it into the barn, but Priscilla quickly told me not to.

She jumped into the buggy with a determined look on her face. "I'm going to find Henry. I can't bear not knowing where he is, or whether or not he's all right."

"But this horse is winded," I protested. "Besides, it might be jittery now and spook for you."

"I don't care if it is winded," Priscilla declared. "If it was fool enough to run off from Henry, he's going to have to run again. And I'll run the jitters out of him." She slapped the lines on the horse's back and went tearing out the lane, gravel and dust flying.

Half an hour later, the same horse and buggy came clip-clopping up the lane, a lot slower this time. Henry was with Priscilla. He dropped her off at the house, turned around, and left right away.

"What happened?" I asked Priscilla when she came in the door.

"Well, I guess it really was Henry's fault," she admitted, half sheepishly. "He stopped in town at the drugstore, drove up to the railing, but didn't bother to tie the horse since he was only planning to stay a minute. When he came out, the horse was gone.

"I met him walking back from town. He said he's learned his lesson, that he'll never again let a horse stand without tying him."

"All's well that ends well," I said. "Isn't it a miracle that the horse didn't run into something or get hit by a car? It could've caused a serious accident."

When Nate came home, I told him about it. He shook his head in disgust and said, "Whew, was that ever dumb! He could've made *dummheide* (caused foolish tricks) yet with the horse running into the traffic like that. Ei yi yi!"

Something made me want to defend Henry, and I said, "Oh well, he's learning fast, and I don't believe he'll make the same mistake twice." ✖

*I*saac and Rosemary spent their last evening and night here before leaving for Minnesota. Beds, bedding, and everything was already packed into the truck, and they needed a place to stay.

They had been planning to stay at her parents' place, but her dad hasn't been well, and they were afraid he wouldn't be able to stand the noise of the children. So Nate told them they could come here.

We spent an enjoyable evening together, gathered around the table, singing hymns, and sometimes just visiting. Grandpa Daves and Henry came, too, and between songs there was no lack of interesting stories. All the babies did well, and I enjoyed the evening immensely.

I wish I could hold on to this evening and never let it go, and that Isaac and Rosemary wouldn't have to leave for far-away Minnesota. I thought of the words of the song, "My dearest friends, in bonds of love, / Our hearts in sweetest union prove; / Your friendship's like a drawing band, / Yet we must take the parting hand" (anon.).

Oh, the glorious hope of someday winning that "happy shore, / Where parting hands are known no more." Matthew came and sat beside me, slipping his hand into mine. I believe there has always been a special place in our hearts for each other, and somewhere, deep down, I'm still "Mammy" to him and he is still my "Sonny Boy."

Yet I know that if they move so far away, the memories will become fainter and fainter, and for him, maybe disappear entirely. There's a pang of sadness in my heart, mingled with the joy of having had him to love for awhile.

Next morning after a breakfast of eggs, mush 'n puddin's, oatmeal with raisins, and fresh milk from the dairy, it was time for them to get ready to go.

Rosemary, eyes bright with unshed tears, came to me and said, "How can I ever thank you well enough for all you've done for Isaac and me? You've truly been a friend in need, and I'm going to miss you so much."

Dear, sweet Rosemary, always so kind and gracious. I hugged her, and our tears flowed freely. If only Minnesota wouldn't be so far away, or if I could at least call her by phone, long distance.

Isaac shook hands with Nate and me, and his voice broke, too, when he bade us good-bye. Then they were off, off to new adventures and experiences and the excitement of moving into a new home.

Our Lord will be with them in Minnesota, same as he is here, and bless them in their endeavors. He has promised, "Lo, I am with you always, even to the end of the world." ✖

*April 7*

*A*lready Baby Sadie is one month old: "Oh, time in thy flight. . ." (Allen). As fast as the wheels of time can hurl us on, we are marching toward eternity. So let us "redeem the time, for the days are evil."

Today was our no-church Sunday, and Priscilla invited Henry for dinner. He keeps us all amused with his attempts at talking Dutch. Actually, he's getting fairly good at it, what with the lessons Priscilla's been giving him.

I marvel at the change in Henry since the first time he was here. He seems much more relaxed and easygoing. I remember thinking him rather stilted and unnatural then.

We had some visitors this afternoon to see the baby. Then tonight, while Nate was choring, an unfamiliar car drove in, and a woman carrying a baby walked to the house. She knocked on the door and asked, "Is this where the Masts live?"

At that moment I recognized her. "Dottie Rogers!" I exclaimed warmly. I invited her in, and we sat in the kitchen talking.

"I'm so desperately lonely," she half moaned. "My husband works during the day and spends his evenings away from home, too. I haven't made any friends yet since we moved here from Virginia.

"It seems so hard that Stacey is a Down's syndrome baby, and it is almost getting the best of me. You were so kind to me at the hospital, . . . and that's why I decided to come and see you." She brushed away a few tears.

"How's Stacey getting along?" I inquired. "Does she let you rest at night?"

"Well, yes, Stacey sleeps a lot of the time, but she's a slow drinker and very placid. I have to wake her for her feedings. She'd sleep five or six hours if I wouldn't wake her.

"Sometimes I wish she wouldn't sleep so much—I get so unbearably lonely. At times I think I won't be able to take another day of it.

"Tony and I were so happy before, . . . but now we hardly ever see each other anymore." She swallowed hard and brushed away a few tears.

What, oh what, could I say to this distraught woman? How would I feel if I had just moved to another state and wouldn't know anyone yet, with no relatives nearby, and even no church people?

"I really think you should start going to church if you haven't done so yet," I suggested. "Maybe you could join a group for young mothers, a morning-for-moms group, or something like that."

Dottie sighed. "I guess you're right. But somehow I haven't felt like taking Stacey out into the public yet. I don't want people to know that she's a Down's syndrome baby." Her sentence ended in a whisper.

"Maybe you haven't accepted her condition yourself yet. I know it's hard, but if you accept it and trust that God has a good purpose he is working out. . . ." I stopped short, remembering what she had said last time.

"No, no," Dottie cried. "Don't say that again. If this is God's will, I don't want to hear about him. If such a thing would be his will, how could he be a loving God?"

Silently I prayed for wisdom to say the right thing, without offending Dottie. Suddenly an inspiration came to me. I told her about Amanda having glutaric acid levels going too high, and how that might affect her body and cause damage.

"You mean you have a handicapped child, too?" Dottie asked in surprise. "Why didn't you tell me before?"

After that, she seemed to relax more in my presence, talking freely, and baring her soul to me. We visited until 9:00 p.m., and she seemed to be reluctant to leave.

"May I come again soon?" she asked, as she was preparing to leave.

"You are more than welcome to come," I assured her. "Wouldn't it be nice, too, if you could go out with your husband sometimes? Maybe you could get a baby-sitter. It would be good for you to start getting out some."

Dottie shook her head. "He never asks me. I think he's glad to get away. But I know I haven't been very good company, either. Many a time he comes home to find me crying. I just can't help it, and he says he can't stand to see me crying all the time."

I wanted to tell her, Try to cheer up, and meet him at the door with a glad smile, and see if it doesn't make a difference. Accept Stacey as she is, and trust in God to help you bear whatever is in store for you.

However, I knew that would sound glib to her. Wouldn't it be nice if she would become a Christian and learn to trust God for everything? I feel so sorry for her—so alone and friendless—and without Jesus as a friend, either. ✖

*Y*esterday one of the ministers and a deacon were here to talk to Priscilla. They have received a complaint about her, and they feel, too, that she and Henry are seeing too much of each other. I've been thinking the same thing myself and feel guilty that I didn't say anything to her.

She sat with downcast eyes as these counselors talked to her. They feel Henry should prove himself as a baptized member of the church before she becomes seriously involved with him.

"But, I've been teaching him Dutch," she protested, looking uncomfortable and red-faced, twisting her handkerchief in her hands.

"Wouldn't it be better if Dave or Annie gave him Dutch lessons?" the deacon asked kindly. "He's there every evening, isn't he?"

"But I—I—want to make him feel welcome among our people," Priscilla said hesitantly. "Maybe he would get discouraged and leave, if I refused to go with him."

"I think he would understand if you would explain it to him. You could still go out with him, maybe once a week, or every two weeks. Be careful and prayerful, and go very, very slowly," Minister Amos advised.

Priscilla seemed quiet and subdued the rest of the day. "They don't trust us," she said dolefully. She stood staring out the window as dusk descended.

"Oh Priscilla, it's not that," I protested. "I think they have good concerns and have your best interests in mind."

Last night Nate and I sat talking until late. It's hard to

know where our duty lies, in giving advice. She's living under our roof, and yet we don't want to meddle in her life unduly.

Then Baby Sadie had one of her rare *gridlich* (grouchy) times, and it was nearly midnight until we got to bed. Just as we were drifting off to sleep, Nate thought he heard a noise outside, and he sat up, wide awake. Then he threw on his clothes and went to investigate, not wanting another of his calves to be stolen.

Fifteen minutes later he returned, looking quite discouraged. "It doesn't look good for Henry," he said, sitting on the bed and resting his head in his hands. "I circled the barn, and out near the road was his buggy with his horse tied to the fence, and no one was around."

"Are you sure it was Henry's rig," I gasped.

Nate nodded. "I had my flashlight, and I'd know his pacer anywhere. I circled the barn again, and a moment later I heard a car start, a piece down the road. When I got back, the rig was moving out, headed in the other direction."

"Was anything stolen?" I asked worriedly.

Nate shook his head, "Not that I could see. By tomorrow I'll be better able to tell if anything's missing."

Sleep was out of the question for us, then, and thoughts tumbled over each other in my mind. Finally, I drifted off into a troubled sleep, dreaming of thieves, and several times I awoke in a terror after a bad dream.

We overslept the next morning and had a late start, which always makes a day seem so hectic.

O God, give us your peace, the peace which passes all understanding. Help us to trust in you and not to worry and fret over our circumstances. Thank you for your loving care and guidance. ✄

*P*riscilla has given Dora a cute, silky Cocker Spaniel puppy for her birthday. He's nice, but what we really need is a good watchdog. Dora named him Cocky, and she sure plays with him a lot.

Today was such a warm balmy spring day, that I decided I just had to go for a walk. I've been cooped up in the house all winter, and I thought it seemed heavenly to get out into the fresh air.

Priscilla put the twins into the twin stroller, and I put Sadie into the baby coach. Dora skipped alongside, with Cocky scampering around her.

The trees along the creek are sprouting green leaves, robins and song sparrows are singing, and daffodils and hyacinths are blooming. I wanted to take great breaths of fresh air, sweet air. Somehow it's easier to appreciate the greatness and majesty and beauty of God's handiwork outdoors.

Yesterday we had a warm rain, and the peas, onions, and radishes are up in the garden, marching in neat little rows. The grass is so green, and everything looks clean and freshly washed after the rain.

For a few moments I felt like hopping, skipping, and jumping, but the urge quickly passed. I need all the energy I have for taking care of my little family.

Nate has been busy plowing these days until the rain stopped him. Then tonight Grandpa Daves and Henry were here for supper—the first time Henry and Priscilla have been together again since the minister and deacon talked to her.

Henry has started going out with an Amish carpenter

crew. After trying it out, he says that's more for him than farming.

He was his usual interesting self this evening, but the thought of him being in our barn the other night kept popping into my mind. Nate found nothing missing the next day, so we decided not to say anything to anyone for the time being.

Grandpa Dave was spouting off about this *dumm* fast time (daylight saving time) that's starting next weekend. Nate said he gripes about it every year.

"It's the stupidest thing I ever heard of," he declared. "You'll never catch me turning my clock ahead one hour! What newfangled notions will they come up with next? God's time is good enough for me! Good old standard time!"

"But next you'll be an hour late when you have a doctor or dentist appointment," Priscilla reminded him.

"Pshaw!" he snorted. "That would serve them right. We don't start church services on fast time, and it's not necessary for the town appointments either."

"Now *Daadi* (Grandpa)," Annie said, putting her hand on his knee. "You must be a good example for our grandchildren." She was holding Baby Sadie, and Dora climbed up onto *Daadi's* lap.

"That's right, that's right," Dave agreed, beaming at the children. "We want them to follow the good old ways, not these worldly notions."

I think Grandpa Dave's bark is worse than his bite, and he really is a good-hearted old soul. He loves the children, and that warms my heart toward him.

Henry and Priscilla left then, to go for a walk, and we sat around the table being entertained by Dave's stories and

Annie's neighborhood news. Our lives are enriched by their friendship and comradeship, and we hope to repay them someday for all they've done for us. ✖

*W*e've had a terrible experience, which gave us all a bad fright. Last week it rained and rained and rained some more. The creek rose until it seemed like a mighty, rushing river, brown and muddy, raging, overflowing its banks like an angry monster. I had never seen it like that before.

While all four of the children were napping, I put on my boots and walked out to get a closer look. It was an awesome feeling, seeing and hearing such mighty power up close.

Occasionally huge logs were swept past, bobbing in the current like matchsticks, and then came a range house, a small portable chicken house. Near the bank lots of debris and a fence post bobbed in the white foamy water.

Nate joined me and asked, almost shouting above the roar of the flood, "Doesn't it make you seem small and helpless?"

I nodded wordlessly. I thought of the mighty power of God and found it comforting to realize that God controls even the floodwaters.

"I haven't seen it like this for at least fifteen years," Nate said. "The *Kette-Schtecke* (swinging bridge) was swept away then, and I'm sure it's gone again. That means I'll have to rebuild it.

"And the water's still rising. Half an hour ago, it was only to the base of the poplar tree. Now it's part way up the trunk."

We watched for several more minutes, feeling almost mesmerized by the water. "Ever notice how, after watching awhile, you yourself seem to be moving instead of the water?" I asked Nate.

He nodded, grinning. "It's a funny feeling. Be careful you don't fall in."

Back in the house, I told Priscilla she ought to go out and see the awesome, wild, raging floodwaters up close, too.

However, she declined, saying that if she hurried, she could make her goal of finishing the housecleaning today. Priscilla has already been energetically scrubbing and cleaning for several weeks and had set today as her goal for having it finished. Where does she get her boundless energy?

Baby Sadie awoke then, and after she had been fed and burped, the twins awoke and wanted to be cuddled for awhile. Dora is usually the first to awaken, and I thought it seemed unusual for her to sleep so long. Finally I went into her room to check on her.

Her bed was empty!

"Priscilla!" I called up the steps. "Is Dora with you?"

"No, I thought she was still napping."

"Come quick," I called. "Watch the babies for me while I run out to see if she's with Nate."

I dashed out toward the barn where he was fixing the corn planter.

"Nate, where's Dora," I shouted urgently.

Hearing the alarm in my voice, he quickly ran over to me. "Isn't she in the house?"

I shook my head. "Please help me hunt for her. She must have slipped out the side door while I was outside and Priscilla was upstairs housecleaning."

Priscilla came to the door, a worried look on her face. "Search the house!" I called to her. "Make sure she's not in a closet or under a bed, or in the attic or cellar."

Now the floodwaters seemed like a menacing enemy. We searched the banks, calling her name. Panic rose within me when I thought of Dora alone near it. The bank was high on our side of the creek, and I shivered uncontrollably.

"O God, help us!" I pleaded out loud, frantically. My voice sounded small and lost in the roar of the mighty rushing water.

Nate had gone downstream, and after I walked a half mile up the creek, searching in vain, I headed back. Maybe he had found her.

Priscilla came out on the back porch and anxiously yelled out to us, "Shall I help search, too?"

"No, just watch the babies," I shouted. "Keep the door closed, and make sure the twins stay inside."

By this time a neighbor on the road had seen us searching and came to help. Soon more searchers arrived. It was a comforting feeling, knowing that others were hunting for Dora, but somehow the whole scene made it seem all the more like a calamity.

I tried to push down my panicky thoughts, to concentrate instead on finding Dora alive and well. I decided to retrace my steps. Maybe a half mile hadn't been far enough. I had gone closer to a mile upstream when I spied a spot of blue ahead. Dora had been wearing a blue dress!

There was Dora!

As I got closer, my heart sank lower and lower. She was lying so still and motionless. And there was Cocky, the puppy, curled up beside her. Her arm was thrown around him.

In a moment my fears were relieved. She was breathing naturally, fast asleep.

"Dora!" I cried joyously, snatching her up and hugging her to myself. I was laughing and crying at the same time.

She looked around, bewildered, her face flushed from sleeping.

"Why did you go out walking?" I chided.

"I didn't want to take a nap," she said in a small voice. "I wanted to take Cocky for a walk."

"But you could've fallen into the water. You must never, never take Cocky for a walk alone."

"The water frightened me," she said, whimpering. "I wanted to find you and Daddy."

I had such a great feeling of relief and happiness in bringing her back to the house safe and sound! The other searchers were informed, and soon they left, relieved that the crisis was past.

My heart has been going out in sympathy to the parents whose little four-year-old son was drowned last summer. Only now am I able to sympathize with them more, but I realize I can't fully feel for them.

I keep claiming the words "My grace is sufficient for you" for whatever may come. I believe God's grace has been sufficient for them, and he is carrying them through their sorrow. ✖

*T*oday I had a letter from Rosemary. It was bubbling over with joy and enthusiasm.

"I like it so much here," she wrote. "I could make myself at home right away. We have a lovely view from our kitchen window—a meadow, trees, a brook, and lots of songbirds singing all day. The road banks are covered with wild roses and honeysuckles, which soon will be in bloom.

"The church group here is friendly, and they gave us a big welcome. It's so peaceful and quiet here. I sure don't miss the traffic and building development going on around us back home.

"On Sunday we went for a walk through our meadow and saw a beaver dam, although with the noise of the children along, we didn't get to see any beavers.

"This Sunday we plan to have church at our house, but with such a small group, getting ready for church isn't near the work it was back home. They all seem like such good friends already. We had a practice singing on Wednesday evening, and it was such an encouragement, such a time of good fellowship."

At the end of her letter, she added, "I hope you and Nate will come out here to visit us sometime. Maybe you'll like it so much you'll want to move here, too! That would be too good to be true."

Well! I'm glad she likes it so well in Minnesota. They are needed there to help make a go of the settlement. But now this fall, a new preacher will have to be ordained here again, to take Isaac's place. We'll be glad when that's over.

Henry has made his application to join our church. He says this is what he wants, to be a part of a group where members do not divorce, where unity and peaceableness abound, where folks are honest and trustworthy, seeking to live holy lives.

I'm not sure we deserve that description. We are all too human and often fall by the wayside. Some have left our people, saying the youth are wild and have low morals. But I feel that's only a justification, an excuse to join a liberal church, to have the modern conveniences they desire.

The truth is, there always does seem to be a wild bunch like that in some communities. It's sad that all the youth are judged because of those few who are disobedient and being a reproach to the church and put us in a bad light before the world.

The majority are seeking to be obedient and doing what's right. They may be babes in Christ, young, easily swayed trees in God's orchard, untrimmed vines in his vineyard. Yet hopefully they are growing in grace until they will be strong, mature Christians, bringing forth fruit for the Lord. We need to show patience.

Judging them all by the wild ones is like Grandpa Dave saying public schools are worthless because a few go through the system without learning to read and figure. However, I really don't know a thing about these big public schools they have today.

I certainly wish Henry well, and I hope he will remain steadfast and true to the faith. He seems so sincere now, but time will tell. I'm sure that many are praying for him, hoping that he will make good and be a stalwart church member, a solid Christian. ✖

*O*h, what a lovely month May *is!* The blossoming fruit trees, spring flowers, green, green grass, refreshing showers, and early garden things. The creek is a gentle stream again. We love to rest in the cool shade of the trees after working in the garden and mowing the lawn.

Dottie Rogers has been coming out to visit at least every week—sometimes oftener. "You're the only friend I have," she told me last time. "If it weren't for you, I'd die of loneliness."

She was here again tonight with Baby Stacey, and as soon as she got out of the car, I noticed that her eyes and face were swollen from crying. We sat on lawn chairs in the yard while she sobbed out her story.

"My husband has left me," she cried in anguish, "for good this time. I knew it was coming, but it's such a shock." Her body shook with sobs.

What could I say to comfort her? If only she could've braced up, accepted Stacey's condition, and been a cheerful wife.

Tony was probably weary of coming home to a pitiful, crying spouse every evening and left to find other companionship. Yet that still doesn't excuse him for leaving. He was the father and husband and needed to encourage his wife, too. They both seemed so young, and this was a heavy burden.

"Oh, Dottie," I finally exclaimed, "if only you could accept Christ as your Savior and friend. There's a song we sing that goes like this:

What a friend we have in Jesus,
   All our sins and griefs to bear.
What a privilege to carry
   Everything to God in prayer.
O what peace we often forfeit,
   O what needless pain we bear,
All because we do not carry
   Everything to God in prayer. (Scriven)

While I sang, Dottie stopped crying and was listening. I took the Bible, turned to Isaiah 53, and read to her: "All we like sheep have gone astray; we have turned every one to our own way; and the Lord has laid on his servant the iniquity of us all."

Then I explained, "Every one of us needs the Savior to rescue us from sin and cleanse us from unrighteousness. Jesus died on the cross and bore the punishment for our sins, so we can be forgiven and restored to fellowship with God.

"When we repent of our sins and ask Jesus Christ to forgive us and take charge of our lives, we can abide in him. Then he is our righteousness, our sin-bearer, and our access to God, so we can fellowship with God as sons and daughters. Through Christ we are adopted into the royal family, redeemed, and made holy, set apart for God."

The setting sun shot long rays over the trees by the creek, and a robin was sweetly singing in the blossoming tree by the garden. I wondered if my words meant anything to Dottie, if something was sinking in, or whether she was utterly confused. At least she was no longer antagonistic. Silently I prayed for wisdom.

"I do believe in God," she finally admitted, scooping up

a kitten that had wandered by her chair. "And I also believe in Jesus as God's Son. My mother was a Christian, and I went to church every Sunday before I got married. But I never prayed or had any kind of a relationship with God.

"You talk of asking Jesus for forgiveness, and also about abiding in Jesus. But what does that mean?"

For a few moments I pondered over this and then replied, "Jesus says, 'I am the vine, you are the branches. The one who abides in me, and I in that one, the same brings forth much fruit; for without me you can do nothing.'

"As a branch in the true vine, we receive spiritual nourishment through the Holy Spirit, just as a branch in a natural vine receives sap and nourishment from it. By ourselves, separate from Christ, we can do nothing good. If a branch breaks off the vine, it no longer receives life from the vine, and so it dies."

"Oh!" Dottie exclaimed, her face lighting up. "I think I'm beginning to understand it now. It sounds like a wonderful, blessed relationship."

"Yes, but before we can have this abundant life, we have to die to self, crucify self with its affections and lusts, and surrender all to God. Even Christians can be lukewarm and carnal. So we have to stay close to Christ."

I wanted to encourage her, but I didn't want to make it sound as though there would be no self-denial and surrendering on our part. So I tried a few more verses.

"Jesus said, 'If any one will come after me, let him deny himself and take up his cross daily and follow me.' Also, 'Whosoever does not bear his cross, and come after me, cannot be my disciple.'

"You have already confessed that you believe in God and that Jesus is his Son. Your next step is receiving him as your Savior and Ruler, forsaking all known sin, and yielding your life to him in obedience and faith," I told her gently.

"Then it will be as if Christ is saying to you, Abide in Me, the heavenly vine. I will receive you, I will draw you to myself, I will give you victory over sin, I will strengthen you and bless you, I will fill you with my Spirit."

"I really would like to have that kind of life," Dottie said wistfully. "But for so long, I've felt that God is far away, that he doesn't care about me, that he is even angry with me. I've felt that way ever since Mother died, five years ago. On her deathbed she told me she was praying for me, that I would yield my life to God and become a Christian."

Dottie paused, swallowing hard. "I prayed for God to spare her life, but God didn't answer my prayer." The tears were flowing again, and Dottie reached for tissues in her purse.

"God's ways are so much higher than our ways," I softly

reminded her. "Sometimes we can't understand why he answers our prayers with a no, or sends us a handicapped child. But we know that all things work together for good to those who love him, and that he is never far away from us.

"Jesus says, 'Come unto me, all you that labor and are heavy laden, and I will give you rest.' He loves you, Dottie, and is yearning after you, knocking on your heart's door. He is not willing that any should perish, but says, 'The one who comes unto me, I will certainly not cast out,' Won't you receive Christ now?"

"I have to think things over first," Dottie said, arising. "I want to be sure that I am ready before I make a decision."

After she had gone, the children were sleeping while Nate and I sat talking under the glow of the moon. The warm, balmy breezes caressed us, and the frogs chorused poignantly from the creek. It was our second anniversary, and neither of us had thought about it until evening.

Nate seemed rather quiet, almost discouraged, and I wondered about it. Was he working too hard? Was the burden of providing for our growing family too much for him? Did he wish he would still be a bachelor?

I decided to solicit his feelings. "Is something bothering you?"

He nodded in the moonlight. "It's the thieves," he replied wearily. "They've struck again. I've just discovered that a lot of my tools are missing from the shop, the most valuable ones."

"Not again," I cried in dismay. "The thought that someone may be targeting us hurts more than the loss of the goods. Why would they do that?"

"I don't know. It is unsettling. I still wonder whether,

somehow, Henry may be involved."

We sat awhile longer, listening to the night insects and the murmuring of the creek. There was turmoil in our hearts, but outside, all was so calm and peaceful.

Inwardly, I cried out to God: Oh, heavenly Father, life is filled with cares perplexing. Help us know what to do about them. Help Dottie to make her decision for you. ✛

*May 17*

*A* soft, spring rain fell all day. We finally got around to butchering our heavy roosters. It would've been better to do it during cold weather, but I wanted to wait until I'd be able to help more.

Grandpa Daves helped and Henry, too. He had off from his carpenter job because of the rain.

Henry really pitched in, with a right good will, scalding, defeathering, singeing, and cutting up the chickens. He's not afraid of hard work but cheerfully embraces it, which I feel is a good sign.

Annie, Priscilla, and I filled two-quart jars with the meat and processed them for three hours in a boiling water bath, using the big furnace kettle in the washhouse. As usual, Dave kept us laughing over his jokes and funny stories. He told of how, when he was in first grade in school, one cold, windy day, the older boys played a mean trick on the younger ones.

"How would you boys like to make a lot of money catching *El-be-drich-lin?*" the big boys asked.

"How would we catch them?" one wanted to know.

"We'll show you at lunchtime. You have to stand at the

corner of a building holding burlap sacks and wait until they fly in. It won't work unless it's cold and windy, like today."

"How much money can we make?" the younger ones asked.

"A whole lot more than you can get for muskrat furs, and even more than you could get for fox hides."

"Can they scratch or bite, or will they spray us like a skunk?" one fearful little boy wanted to know.

"No, no!" The older boys roared with laughter. "You won't have to be afraid of them."

"What do they look like? Do they have big ears or sharp teeth and claws?"

"Wait until you catch them, then you'll see." They made it sound mysterious.

"At noon the boys ate their lunch in ten minutes, then ran out to the outhouse. The bigger ones had brought sacks along, which they now took out of hiding. It was nearly the coldest day of the year, the chill factor at about zero.

"Before the big boys went inside, they showed the little boys where to stand at the corner of the outhouse. There they were, shivering in the wind's icy blast, holding open their sacks.

"I was freezing, chust freezing," Dave said. "But I thought I could stand it as long as the others could. Besides, I was thinking of all the money I'd make.

"When the bell finally rang, we were so cold that we stood shivering and crying around the big potbellied stove in the middle of the schoolroom, trying to get warm. When the teacher discovered the dirty trick the big boys had played on us, he used the strap on them.

"It served them right. Don't ever let anyone play the *El-be-drich-lin* joke on you," he said teasingly to Henry. "There's no such thing."

Dave had more stories. "Then there was the time my horse had the distemper. So to go to the singing, I borrowed my cousin Abe's horse. Abe lived a half mile down the road and had gone to another county for the weekend. I knew he wouldn't be using his horse, anyhow, so I borrowed the whole rig, harness, buggy, and all.

"Well, it so happened that Abe came home earlier than planned and got off the van right at the singing, figuring he could catch a ride home with his brother.

"I guess I had a pretty big mouth even then," Dave admitted, "and a bunch of the boys decided to play a joke on me. I later found out it was all Abe's idea.

"They knew where I had tied 'my' horse, so they sneaked over to it in the dark and took off the harness. Abe never noticed that it was *his* horse, and they took apart that harness piece by piece and chucked some of the pieces up into a tree, threw some parts into the water trough and up on the barn roof, and even into the steer pen.

"Then they all hid in the hayloft with their flashlights to watch me when I find the harness gone and laugh at me when I try to put it together again," Dave chuckled.

"As soon as I saw what they'd done, I knew it was one of Abe's ideas. Ha! Ha! That was one joke that really boomeranged. I was the one who got the ride home with Abe's brother, and Abe had all night to put his own harness back together.

"He who laughs last, laughs best," Dave chortled. "If you dig a pit for someone else to fall in, watch out; likely you'll end up in the pit yourself. Ha! Ha!"

Dave sure enjoyed telling that story, and he entertained us all day. Annie managed to get some neighborhood gossip in edgewise, though, and she told us that Junior Miller's cow had died, and that Levi Mary had a sprained ankle, and that Ben's Elam's Rebecca had quit her boyfriend.

As they were leaving, Annie asked, "Did you hear that Abner Miller's Emma had the highest score on her achievement test in the whole township? Imagine that! The whole township! I always knew the Millers were smart. . . ."

"Hmph!" snorted Dave. "She didn't have to be very smart to be smarter than them public school kids."

Priscilla rolled her eyes around as if to say, *There we go again.*

"Each to his own opinion," I told her softly.

She whispered back, "He's in his second childhood."

Henry overheard and chuckled. "We love him anyway," he whispered back.

It was a satisfying feeling to see all those jars of chicken meat lined up on the washhouse floor, tonight, ready for quick, tasty meals.

As I got the twins ready for their baths tonight, I felt richly blessed, surrounded by loved ones.

There was Dora by my side, ready to hand me the soap and towels when I needed them, chattering brightly all the while. Peter, cute and chubby, the picture of health, splashing in the water, smiling mischievously. Amanda, sweet and demure as ever, and Baby Sadie in her little seat, waiting contentedly for her evening feeding.

Priscilla was in the kitchen, singing while making rhubarb pies, and Nate out in the barn doing chores, working hard to provide for his little family.

I thought of Dottie Rogers being all alone, her husband

gone, and having a hard time accepting her baby as she is, maybe even now, crying again.

I paused to pray for her, that she might yield her life to Christ, that her husband would come back and find a changed and happy wife, that they both might become Christians and love each other again. ✖

*June 15*

*T*oday was one of those rare, lovely days again—so beautiful—almost like a foretaste of heaven. It's time for roses and honeysuckle, and the peas and strawberries are in full swing.

During this busy season, what would I do without Priscilla? I know how hectic and rushed things would be if I'd have to do it all myself. She picks the berries and cans them, picks the peas and *blicks* (shells) them and prepares them for the locker, makes strawberry pies and shortcake.

Today she drove to town for ice and made a freezer full of delicious strawberry ice cream, hand churned. Her boundless energy and enthusiasm is amazing!

All day I hadn't once thought of my birthday coming up tomorrow, Sunday, until at the supper table. Then Priscilla came in with a decorated cake and the ice cream, singing "Happy birthday to you."

Oh, my! Forty-five already! Sometimes I wish I could hold back the hands of time. The years just fly by so fast. I guess when we're busy and happy, time goes too fast. When we're ill or miserable, it seems to stand still.

Today I received another letter from Polly, and I just had to laugh until the tears rolled down my cheeks when I read her news. I don't know why it struck me so funny, maybe because I remember her telling me that she won't be able to have any children, and that I'll probably have half a dozen!

Polly's "change of life" symptoms turned out to be a change-of-life baby.

She seemed positively awed. "I'll be fifty in a few years, Miriam," she wrote. "I just can't believe it. Sometimes I actually pinch myself to see if I'm dreaming. I was so sure it would never happen."

Polly still seems to be wearing her rose-colored glasses, and I'm happy and excited for her. I can hardly wait. Even though she has seven stepchildren, her own child will be very precious, I'm sure. ✖

$W$e had our first meal of Silver Queen sweet corn. Hmmmm, delicious! And Priscilla found the first ripe tomato, an Early Girl hybrid. She keeps the garden spotless and weedfree, and I know she is spoiling me.

Actually, I should be working outside more, getting more exercise. Just this morning I stepped on the scales and noticed that I have to lose at least ten pounds of what I call "baby fat." Immediately I decided that I simply must go on a diet. Then this afternoon Priscilla baked whoopee pies, and I decided to wait until tomorrow. Sigh!

Today Nate came home from the sale barn with a big, savage-looking brute of a dog. Someone offered it to him, free. He's supposed to be a good watchdog and safe around children, but he almost gives me the shivers. He looks so fierce.

Nate had gone to the sale barn in hopes of buying a horse but found none that suited him. His faithful old sorrel horse finally gave out, going lame in one front leg. Nate had gotten Sorrel as a colt when he began his *rum-schpringe* (running-around) years and kept him ever since. He must be over thirty years old, a remarkable age for a horse. Most horses don't last nearly that long.

Now old Sorrel is out on the meadow. Nate wants him to have a peaceful retirement, to die a natural death, in dignity and honor. I can tell that there's a strong bond between him and his horse, a strong attachment. I hope we'll be able to find another horse, one that suits us just as well. ✖

*D*ottie spent the evening here again. She's hungering after God but not ready to make a decision yet. Her husband is keeping in touch with her, but so far, he hasn't come back. Baby Stacey is doing well and seems like such a sweet baby. Her eyes look almost oriental, and she's small for her age.

We were really worried about Amanda these last few days. She had a bad case of diarrhea, and we knew that could lead to dehydration which could cause her glutaric acid levels to go up. We hired a driver and made a quick trip to the specialist.

He told us to give her plenty of liquids and doses of baking soda, and she's a lot better now. I guess we'll never really completely relax about her health.

We'll love her while we have her, and we try to make the best of things. Life is fragile for all of us, but we realize that for Amanda, it is more so.

Nate was mowing hayfields today, and I saw him anxiously scanning the sky. He's hoping the hay won't get rained on.

I like the sweet fragrance of new-mown hay that comes wafting on the breeze in the warm sunshine, the swallows twittering and darting in and out of the barn, the picturesque pink and white petunias blooming by the mailbox, the fast-growing cornfields. Ah, sweet summertime in the country! ✖

*T*here is no greater task than that of being a parent. Sometimes the awesomeness of parenthood is almost overwhelming. Such innocent little souls are entrusted to our care, souls that will live for all eternity. Such a big responsibility! The knowledge that I am a weak, imperfect parent is almost staggering.

O God, give me the wisdom I need to discipline wisely, never in anger. Help me to live so that if my children model me, they will have a beautiful character and personality. Help me to keep their little emotional tanks filled to the brim with love, and to instill within them a sense of self-worth and belonging.

Let me tell them Bible stories and speak of your wondrous creations of nature—birds, flowers, trees, stars. Shape my life and words to speak of your wondrous love, so they think of you as the Giver of all good things, with infinite care and provision. Amen.

Children need warm, outgoing affection daily. They all need the comforting arm of love even when they do not deserve it. In fact, they need it most of all then, as much as they need food and fresh air.

Children need praise and appreciation, and if they do not receive it, they will search for it in odd, sometimes hurtful ways. If we want to help others become beautiful people, we should work at it through sincere praise and encouragement. We all need warmth and tenderness to change for the better. Let each day be a hunting trip—hunting for something good in each child to compliment and give sincere praise for.

Lord, teach us patience while the little hands
Engage us with their ceaseless small demands.
Oh, give us gentle words and smiling eyes
And keep our lips from hasty, sharp replies.
Let not weariness, confusion, and noise
Obscure our vision of life's fleeting joys.
Then, when in years to come, our house is still,
No bitter memories its rooms shall fill.
(author unknown)

O God, undertake for me. ✖

*July 29*

Sweet summer days are passing in swift succession. Old Sorrel died this afternoon. We found him lying peacefully in the meadow, surrounded by mists of the morning and songs of the lark. Nate couldn't eat much breakfast. To him, it was the loss of an old friend. The horse we now have is not doing well. We're thinking of getting rid of it and buying another one.

This afternoon two men from the Calvary Baptist church came to the door. Nate talked with them on the porch, and I could hear the conversation from inside, where I was *blicking* (shelling) lima beans. Apparently they were out soul-winning.

"If you were to die tonight," one of the men asked Nate, "are you sure you would go to heaven?"

He replied, "I am trusting in Christ for my salvation, and I would hope to attain heaven."

"Oh, but you can be sure, not merely hope so," the man

replied. "I feel sorry for you people, trying to earn your way into heaven by your good works and your traditions. You'll never make it that way.

"Christ has done everything on Calvary. He told us, 'It is finished.' There is nothing more for us to do besides accepting the gift of salvation by faith. We can't earn salvation by trying to be good enough or doing enough good works."

"You're right," Nate agreed. "But I believe you've been misinformed about us. We are not trying to earn our salvation. That would be impossible. Our only hope is in the shed blood of Christ. But we do have conditions to meet, and that is to believe that Jesus is God's Son and that he is the expiation for our sins. We need to forsake all known sin and follow Jesus."

"But aren't you trying to earn your salvation by wearing plain clothes and doing without modern conveniences?"

"Oh, no," Nate replied quickly. "Those things will never earn salvation for anyone. We're trying to obey God by wearing modest, full-length clothes, and we feel it's a sin to be scantily clad, or to wear clothes that cause pride and attract attention to our bodies. In our opinion, many human inventions lead people away from God and into a life of ease and luxury and temptations."

The men left soon after, apologizing for their misconceptions.

Cocky and Rusty, the new dog, came up from the meadow just then, where they had been chasing rabbits. Rusty gave them a vicious send-off. He's an excellent watchdog but a nuisance in a case like that. We're afraid he might bite someone sometime. But nothing has been stolen since we got him. ✄

*H*enry took Priscilla for a drive tonight, and when she returned, she flopped down on the settee and burst into tears.

"What's wrong, Priscilla?" I cried in alarm. "What happened?"

"It's Henry," she cried petulantly. "He can be so adamant. He doesn't think it will be a good idea for us to take Dora when we get married. He thinks she should stay with you."

Relief flooded through my being. "Has Henry talked of marriage already?" I asked.

"Not really. I guess we're both taking it for granted. Next month he will be baptized, and then we can plan. But he's refusing to budge on the matter of raising Dora.

"After all, she *is* my daughter," Priscilla exclaimed indignantly. "I should have some say in it, I think."

*Good for Henry!* I was thinking.

To Priscilla, I said, "Have you prayed about it? Are you seeking God's will in the matter?"

"Well, no, I haven't," she slowly admitted. "I was so sure that I have a right to Dora. And I'd like to raise her as my daughter."

She went upstairs then, and as I sat on the rocker breast-feeding Baby Sadie, my eyes followed Dora while she played with her doll. She's getting lovelier every day.

Am I fit to be a mother to a girl like this? Will she have struggles with pride, or temptations to flirt, or think herself better than others? That would be worse than being homely and struggling with feelings of inferiority and low self-worth.

O Lord, guide us all, and lead Henry and Priscilla to the right decision. Help Priscilla to give up her own will in the matter if Henry refuses to take Dora. ✖

*August 22*

$P$eter is such an active little fel-low. He climbs up on chairs, takes all my kettles out of the cupboards to play with, and gets into lots of things he shouldn't. If Priscilla wouldn't be here, I'd have to get a *Maud* (maid) this summer.

Amanda usually sits quietly and plays for long hours at a time. She's so sweet and contented. If Peter comes and grabs one of her toys, she simply picks up something else to play with.

Dora and Peter get into scraps with each other sometimes, but never with Amanda. Nate calls her his little angel.

Sadie can almost sit up by herself now if propped with pillows. Tonight I put her and Amanda in the baby coach and wheeled them into the garden. There I could keep an eye on them while I picked lima beans. Priscilla had taken Dora and Peter and the dogs for a walk.

A few minutes later, a car pulled into the barnyard, and a man and a woman came walking toward me. At first I didn't recognize them—they both looked so radiantly happy. It was Dottie and Tony Rogers.

"How nice to see you together again," I welcomed them, smiling.

"I came home and found that Dottie was a new person," Mr. Rogers said gratefully. "She was so joyous. Then she told me that she had accepted Christ and that was what made her so happy."

Dottie nodded. "I was able to lead him to Christ, too." Her voice pulsated with gladness. "Now we are one, in Christ."

"I'm so happy for you," I said simply. "The day of miracles is not yet past."

"Thank you for helping my wife," Tony said. "We've found a Bible-believing church, the one my parents attend, and we are planning to be baptized soon. They've been praying for this for quite a while."

"God does answer prayers," I rejoiced with them.

After they had left, I thought things over. *Just maybe God used a Down's syndrome baby to bring them to him.*

Maybe it was the only way he could get their attention. God sometimes "moves in a mysterious way his wonders to perform" (Cowper). ✖

*T*oday I had another enthusi-astic letter from Rosemary. She says they still like their new home and haven't had a day of homesickness yet. They're having picture-perfect weather just now, but we're in the midst of a heat wave. It hasn't rained for three weeks. The creek is lower than I've ever seen it before.

This forenoon, at my request, Nate got the old boat down. We loaded it with empty boxes and baskets and headed upstream looking for elderberries. They grow on bushes along the banks and can be picked from the boat.

What a lot of memories came flooding back! There was the time I was going boating with Nate before we were married.

Those days, I still thought I was keeping company with Nate to provoke Hannah to jealousy. I was determined that no one would ever find out that I loved Nate.

It's uncanny sometimes, the way Nate seems to read my thoughts. Just then he asked, "Remember the time you ran away from me and fell into the water and nearly drowned?"

"So that's how you exaggerate things!" I was laughing. "Actually, I nearly drowned in my own tears!"

We talked and reminisced about those pretending-courtship days as we picked the juicy purple berries. A few late summer birds were chirping in the trees, and it was so peaceful and serene there on the water.

After we had filled our containers, we headed back, refreshed by the beauty and calmness of nature. What a contrast between now and the way it was during the flood in April.

Priscilla and I had a busy day ahead, canning *Hollerbier* (elderberry) juice and making *Hollerbier* jelly and pies. Hmmmmm! What tastes better?

When we reached the house, an irate neighbor, Eli, was waiting for us. He reported that twenty of his prize leghorn hens were killed last night, right out of their pens. He has a suspicious eye on Rusty, claiming it couldn't have been just any young pup. An experienced killer must have done it, for they heard no commotion or squawking whatsoever.

Nate promised that from now on, he would keep Rusty penned in the barn at night. If the killing continues, then we'll know it wasn't Rusty. He's such a good watchdog and so far has kept the thieves away. I hope he's proven innocent.

*September 22*

We just heard the wonderful news today, that Allen and Polly have a little son named Daniel. Now I'm hankering to visit and see the little fellow. I can hardly believe that Polly has a baby of her own. If only our horse would do a little better.

Last Sunday was the long-planned-for day when Henry was baptized and taken into the church as a member, along with the other applicants. We wanted to be at church bright and early, but then our stupid horse balked at a crossing, when we were halfway there. He just simply refused to budge another inch.

Nate tapped him with the whip, but that only irritated him. Then he got out to lead him, but he planted his four feet firmly on the ground and refused to move. Next Nate got back in and gave him a lash with the whip. That got him really angry, and he threatened to throw himself on the ground.

So we sat and waited and waited. It seemed like an hour. My patience was wearing as thin as it possibly could. I became so irritable and upset and in a bad mood. I felt like taking the biggest rock I could find and throwing it at the beast.

Finally (it was only fifteen minutes later) another horse and buggy came up behind us. When they passed us, our horse started up, too, and followed along to the farm where services were being held.

I hope Nate sends that horse to the butcher to be made into dogfood next week!

The baptismal services were soul-satisfying and inspiring, and my bad feelings evaporated. Henry has a humble, submissive attitude, and he is in line with the *Ordnung* (rules) of the church.

Priscilla seemed radiantly happy all afternoon. Will she ask us to have her wedding at our house in November? The thought makes me feel tired already. I've been fighting nausea and weariness these last few weeks, which makes me think there's another March baby on the way.

Already I'm worrying about how I'll manage without Priscilla. She'll probably be married by then. Four babies in three years' time!

When I told Nate, he merely said, in a teasing voice, "Well, we've got to make hay while the sun shines, and we haven't got much time left."

It's true. I know I'll soon be too old, and in the long run, it's better for the children to be close together. But it's the short run that's hard. I feel like I could be seventy years old now already! ✖

*October 23*

*T*he last few weeks have been busy ones, with the cornhusking and other fall work. At least the ordination is over now, so that's off our minds.

A new minister has been ordained in Isaac's place, twenty-eight-year-old Emanuel Yoder, chosen by lot. He and his wife both took it quite hard, and I'm sure many a prayer was sent heavenward on their behalf.

Henry came over tonight, and he and Priscilla walked off together along the creek, under the glorious display of dying leaves, golds, browns, and crimson. She looked young and beautiful, and Henry, tall and handsome.

Ah, young love! I felt a little stab of jealousy pierce my heart. They were so carefree and radiant. By contrast, I felt worn out, weary, tied down, cooped up in the house.

An hour later they returned. Nate had finished the chores and sat reading *Farm Journal* with Baby Sadie snuggled in his arms. The other children were already sleeping, and I was working on a quilt patch Grandma Annie had given me to put into a friendship quilt for a new family in the neighborhood.

The door opened, and Henry and Priscilla walked in.

Priscilla was positively glowing, her cheeks were pink, and her eyes sparkling. *She's the picture of health and beauty,* I thought.

Henry—how he has changed since I first saw him nearly a year ago. Then he was thin and pale; now he has filled out, probably from the hard work and Pennsylvania Dutch cooking. He looks like a real Amishman with his plain clothes.

His manner and bearing have changed. Somehow he seems a lot more confident. I remember thinking him a bit shifty-eyed the first time I saw him, but now he has a confident, wholesome air about him.

At our invitation, they seated themselves on the settee, and Henry cleared his throat. "We have decided to be married the first week in December."

Priscilla added, "And we'd like to know if we can have the wedding here at your house."

Only about six weeks from now! Would we ever be able to get ready in time?

"Of course," Nate consented, "if it's okay with Miriam." He looked toward me.

I nodded, all smiles. "With Priscilla here, we'll be able to manage. She has enough energy for two people."

Henry chuckled at that. "I'll help, too," he offered. "My carpenter work will be slowing down over the cold winter weather anyhow."

"There's another thing," Priscilla added. "We've both decided that it would be best to let Dora stay with you."

I thought, *So she has given up her own will in the matter—how grand of her!*

Priscilla went on, "We know she'll have a good upbringing here, with you for mother and dad."

"Well . . . thank you," I managed to say, completely overwhelmed by her generosity and kindness.

Nate promised, "We'll do our best to give her a good home and raise her well. And we hope you'll be able to come and see her often."

"That's another thing," Henry said. "We'd like to stay near her and all of you. Do you know of any houses for rent in this area? We'd like to be in this church district, too, if possible."

We promised to be on the lookout for a place for them to rent, since we'd sure like to have them living close by.

After Henry had left and Priscilla had gone to bed, Nate and I sat talking and reminiscing until late. Somehow, we now feel sure that Henry had nothing to do with the stealing taking place on our farm, and that he's entirely trustworthy and sincere.

Henry has proved himself an honest man, a real Christian, and will make a stable husband for Priscilla.

"Surely goodness and mercy shall follow them all the days of their lives, and they shall dwell in the house of the Lord forever." ✖

*November 21*

$O$h, how swiftly things can change in a short time! I can hardly bear to even write down what happened since the last time I wrote in here.

Priscilla was so happy, working hard, singing wherever she went, while helping to get the fall work done—corn-husking, housecleaning, baby-sitting. . . . Until the terrible evening when Grandpa Daves drove in with the bad news.

They were driving slowly, and even the horse hung his head.

I knew right away something was wrong. For one thing, they were both awful quiet, which in itself is an indication that something's dreadfully amiss.

Priscilla was working in the garden, digging the last of the carrots, and didn't join us, which was a good thing.

Annie began to cry softly as Dave told us that Henry had not come down to breakfast that morning. They assumed he had gone to work without eating breakfast, as he sometimes does. But when he didn't come home for supper at the usual time, they knew something was wrong and went to his room to investigate.

Henry's bed was neatly made, and on top was an envelope with their names written on it.

Dave got the letter out of his pocket, and handed it to us. "Read it yourself," he said gruffly, trying to hide his emotions.

With trembling hands I pulled the sheet out of the envelope and read it out loud so Nate could hear.

Dear Dave & Annie,

I'm going far away. Please tell Priscilla that I can't marry her after all—I just can't bear to tell her myself. Please break the news gently to her.

I did not know until yesterday that I would not be able to marry in the Amish church if my first woman is still living.

Two years ago she took our baby daughter and left me. Now she is married to another man. I still want to remain in the Amish church, but now I know that I can never marry while she is still living.

I know I'll have to move far away from Priscilla—I couldn't bear to be near her. Tell her I still love her, and always will. I just wish someone had told me sooner.

Henry

There was a moment of stunned silence. Then I blurted out, "But he had Priscilla under the impression that he was never married."

"That's what I thought, too," Dave said. "Remember the time I asked him why a good-looking chap like him hadn't gotten married yet?"

Annie nodded. "And he replied, 'Nobody ever asked me.' "

"Well, we'll leave it to you to tell Priscilla," Dave suggested gently. "You're closer to her than we are."

Annie reached out and clasped my hand. "God will help her to bear it," she murmured, wiping away her tears. They drove off, leaving us standing there, heartsick and afraid, holding Henry's letter.

"I can't bear telling her, either," I moaned in an anguished voice. "You'll have to do it, Nate."

"Maybe we could wait to tell her until tomorrow morning. Perhaps Henry will come back," he said hopefully.

We finally decided to wait till morning to tell her, so she could first get a good night's sleep. Neither of *us* slept a wink, though.

In the morning when Priscilla came skipping down the steps, pinning on her apron and humming a happy tune, I felt like a cruel, heartless person, about to destroy her happiness. What was it she had called me once? A killjoy? That surely described Nate and me now.

Priscilla turned pale as death as she read the letter. She

swayed slightly, and for a moment I thought she would faint and fall over in a heap. She didn't cry out, she didn't say a word, but her eyes looked tortured and haunted, like deep orbs of anguish. I couldn't bear to look at them.

She crossed the kitchen to the range, grabbed the stove lifter, raised the lid, and tossed the letter into the flames. Then she turned and went up the steps to her room. I followed her and found her huddled pitifully in her bed, the picture of abject misery and dejection.

"Just leave me alone," she muttered wearily, and covered her head with a quilt.

That's where she's been spending most of her time ever since. People have been in and out, wanting to visit her and cheer her, but she turns her face to the wall. She eats hardly enough to keep alive, and yesterday when I took a bit up to her, she said in an anguished voice, "If only I could cry, I might feel better. But I can't. Even that is denied me."

I thought of Dottie, how she couldn't stop crying, and now Priscilla was wishing she *could* cry. It was all very confusing.

"But you can pray," I reminded her. "You don't have to bear this alone."

She shook her head. "Where is God?" she asked dumbly. "He has deserted me just when I need him the most."

"No," I replied. "I think it's natural for Christians to feel that way when misfortune strikes them, to feel that God is angry or doesn't love them anymore. That's exactly the way Isaac felt when—" I stopped suddenly, but it was too late.

Priscilla sat up hastily, wide-eyed, remembering. "Oh!" she gasped. "I never realized what I had put him through.

Now I *know* I deserve this, that God is punishing me for what I did to Isaac."

"No, no!" I protested, more sharply than I intended to. "God doesn't punish anyone after he has forgiven them. Often the natural consequences of sin do follow, but it's not that in this case. Just keep on trusting God—trusting that all things work together for good to those who love him. The Lord has promised to never leave you nor forsake you."

I paused, and after a few moments of shared silence and suffering, I added,

"Do you remember the story about the man who had a

dream of walking along the beach with the Lord? The scenes of his life flashed before him, and in looking back he noticed that during the lowest and saddest times in his life, there was only one set of footprints in the sand. He questioned the Lord about it: 'I don't understand why, when I needed you most, you left me.'

"And the Lord replied, 'My precious, precious child, I love you, and would never leave you during your times of trial and suffering. Where you see only one set of footprints, that was when I carried you.' "

That seemed to be the turning point for Priscilla, toward emotional healing, and I'm hoping it will last. She got dressed then, came downstairs, and visited a bit with Grandpa Dave and Grandma Annie. She attempted to help a little with the work. She's trying to be brave and to force herself to be cheerful. It nearly breaks my heart, watching her. ✖

*December 26*

*J*oy to the world! the Lord is come! / Let earth receive her King; / Let every heart prepare him room, / And heaven and nature sing" (Watts).

In spite of that blessed hope of eternal joy, yesterday was a rather cheerless Christmas Day at our house. One bright spot, though, was the happiness Grandpa Dave and Grandma Annie showed in giving gifts to their "grandchildren" for the first time.

For Dora, Annie had made a life-size doll in Cabbage Patch style, fully dressed, even to pantaloons and petticoats, but without face markings, in our Amish way. I really don't know who was the happiest, the giver or the receiver. Dora's eyes simply shone with happiness, and the doll has been her constant companion ever since.

As a gift for Peter, Dave had cut out some wooden farm animals with a scroll saw and painted them. For Amanda and Sadie, there were small rag dolls, just as neatly dressed as Dora's big doll.

Priscilla excused herself and went to her room, which somehow dampened all our spirits. Grandpa and Grandma left early.

Soon after they had gone, there were loud knocks on the door and angry shouts from the porch. It was the neighbors who last year had moved into the trailer in the woods, a half mile down the road, a man and his two teen-aged sons.

"We just discovered your dog in our rabbit pen, killing our rabbits in broad daylight," the man barked, red-faced and angry. The purple veins stood out on his forehead and on his bald head.

"Those rabbits were worth $5.00 each, and he killed eleven of them!" The man was actually quivering with anger.

"I put a bullet through his head," the man went on. "Now are you going to hand over the $55.00, or shall I do the same to you?" He took a menacing step forward.

I shivered involuntarily. Those boys often roared down the road on their three-wheelers, shattering the peace of the countryside and sometimes tearing into the fields and damaging crops.

"I'm sorry, I don't have $55.00 in cash," Nate calmly replied. "But I can write you a check. Will that be satisfactory?"

"Hand it over then," the man growled, somewhat mollified. When he left, check in hand, he called back over his shoulder, "You'll find your dog out behind the barn."

That was where Nate found Rusty's body when he went out to chore. "At least I was spared the task of shooting him," Nate told me later. "Now I guess I'll have to pay for Eli's twenty leghorns, too, for I'm almost sure it was Rusty who killed them, if he also killed those rabbits."

It sure spites me (I'm sorry) about our watchdog. Oh well, maybe Cocky will keep the thieves away.

Last night when I stepped outside into the frosty air to feed the cats, I heard a group of carolers going by on a tractor-drawn hay wagon. They were singing heartily, and the happy strains of "We wish you a merry Christmas" came floating back to me. Merry? Not exactly. ✖

# *Reunions*

*January 8*

*P*riscilla has seemed tired and listless these last few weeks.

"Every chair pulls me down as I walk past it," she moaned yesterday. "I know I should help you more, but. . . ."

"I think you should see a doctor," I told her emphatically. "Will you let Nate go to the phone and make an appointment for you?"

She shook her head. "I think it's just because I have so little enthusiasm for living. I'm plain lazy. It's all in my head." She laughed a dry, mirthless laugh.

"Do you mind if we ask Dr. Wing to make a house call, to see you here at home? Maybe he could give you something to make you feel peppier."

"No, don't do that!" she objected. "It doesn't matter to me whether I live or die."

"Priscilla!" I cried, shocked. "Don't talk like that!"

"I'll lie down awhile, and then I'll feel better," she replied, and then curled up on the settee.

She slept until suppertime. When she awoke and tried to walk to the table, she fainted and fell to the floor. We could not revive her, and I felt the same helpless panic that had washed over me three years ago when I'd found Nate alone in the dark, sick and helpless from food poisoning.

I knew I had to remain calm so I wouldn't frighten the children, but I felt like crying or screaming. Nate went for help, and a short time later Priscilla was in an ambulance, headed for the hospital. The doctors are still doing tests, and I'm wondering, *Will they be able to heal a broken heart?*

Now I am worrying about finding someone to be my *Maud* (maid) in March, when our baby comes. It's high time I found someone. I had been depending on Priscilla feeling well enough by then, but now I doubt it. Whatever her trouble is, I feel sure she'll need plenty of bed rest for quite a while.

On top of all our other troubles, the thieves struck again last night. About ten bags of calf vealer feed have disappeared, and there was a note stuck on the barn wall, with a few bad words written on. It makes me feel awful, and Nate seems discouraged, too.

O God, help us to be of good courage. ✖

*January 15*

We've just come back from visiting Priscilla at the hospital. She seems as tired as ever. The doctor told us her blood levels are critical—her red cells, hemoglobin, and platelets are all very low, while her white cells are too high.

It's the same problem she's had before. But this time her body, or her immune system, is doing nothing to fight the condition. "She seems to have lost her will to live," the doctor told us in the hall.

I went to her bed and clasped her hand. "Remember when you told me you were taking Jesus as your Healer?" I whispered.

She shook her head and murmured dispiritedly, "It's not always God's will to heal."

So now the tables are turned. That time she had been the one to tell *us* that Jesus heals, and Nate told her it's not always God's will. Now she has lost her faith. All my efforts to cheer her proved fruitless. We left with heavy hearts.

Big, wet snowflakes were falling when we walked out of the hospital to the neighbor's car. The roads were slippery and dangerous, and we prayed for a safe trip home. A mile from home, where our country road turns off the highway, we came upon an accident. A big trailer truck had hit and killed a horse.

"It must've been a runaway," Nate observed, peering through the snowy window.

I shivered. Just one more mile, then we'd be safe home. We picked up the children at Grandpa's, and then, finally, we were at home.

"What in the world!" Nate exclaimed, and sprang from the car. The big double barn doors were standing wide open. The door to the horse's stall was open, too, and the horse was gone. There was another nasty note on the same nail.

So, after helping to get the children to the house, Nate went with the neighbor again, back to the scene of the accident. He needed to talk to the truck driver—for there was no doubt in our minds that it was our "Old Balker" that was killed.

It surely doesn't spite me for him (I'm not sorry to be rid of him), but I really wish he wouldn't have been killed in such a way. ✖

*I*'ve finally found myself a *Maud* (maid) for March, and that's a load off my mind. It's seventeen-year-old Barbianne Fisher, and she can stay as long as we need her.

That's the good news. The bad news is from the driver of the truck that killed our horse. He was here yesterday and presented us with a bill of $7,000 for damage to the front of his rig. All the strength went out of my legs. I was glad there was a chair nearby.

Nate's been thinking of sitting up in the barn some night with a bright flashlight, to try to find out who the culprits are. But I've been trying to dissuade him. They might be dangerous characters or even carrying guns. If I were to meet one of them, would I be able to remember that behind the face of every person, we can see the face of Jesus, and we can hear him say, "I died for that person"? ✖

*T*he red-winged blackbirds are back! I feel like rejoicing—it's usually the first sign of spring. Priscilla is at home, and we've set up a bed in the sitting room for her. She's somewhat better, but still weak and tired.

Someone put a note in *Die Botschaft* (The message; a periodical) announcing a shower for her. So she's been receiving lots of cards and letters, which are a great pastime for her. Words of good cheer and good wishes seem to help her a lot.

One letter that really impressed me was from a young widow whose husband drowned when the tractor he was driving rolled over into a pond and he was trapped underneath. (They are New Amish and use tractors.) On her card she had written this verse:

> I do not ask to be set free,
>     From sorrow, care, and pain;
> But trusting Jesus, I'll press on,
>     That heavenly home to gain.
> May he take me by the hand,
>     And help me through this day;
> Then, trusting him, I'll smile again,
>     And work and love and pray.

We had another visit from neighbor Eli this morning, and he was even more irate than last time. When he went out to the chicken house, he found lots of his leghorns mercilessly killed and strewn about. He blurted out to Nate, "That dog of yours must've been on the loose again last night!"

Eli sure changed his tune when Nate told him that Rusty had been dead since Christmas Day. Maybe it wasn't Rusty after all, who killed those other twenty leghorns.

I had a doctor appointment today, and it looks like I'll be able to have my wish this time—a home delivery! I'm so glad. The doctor even kindly recommended a midwife for me, and it was the same one that Polly had when her baby was born. In a letter to me, she described how kind, helpful, gentle, and understanding this midwife was, and how it made things easier for her. I can hardly wait! ✖

*March 1*

*A* scrawny little chap by the name of Crist joined our family in the early morning hours today. He just weighed a little over five pounds, and he doesn't look like anyone in the family.

When I first saw him, I thought the only word to properly describe him would be elfin. He looked just like a little elf. But there's nothing elfin about his lusty yell. I believe he was born with a bellyache. It really was nice to have a home delivery. The midwife arrived just in time, and she was all that Polly described her to be. I feel like I've made a new friend.

Barbianne Fisher came soon after we sent word over to her. I feel slightly put out with her tonight. She's in the barn helping Nate with the chores, but no one told her to go. The supper dishes aren't washed, and the kitchen hasn't been swept today. She told me she detests housework and would rather work outside any day.

Oh well, she *is* good with the children. She bundled them up and took them along out. Priscilla slipped on her housecoat and walked over from her bed in the sitting room to see little Crist, with me in our bedroom. I thought she seemed brighter and stronger, almost as if a spark of her old enthusiasm would be returning.

When I lamented the fact that the kitchen looks a sight, I

thought I saw a hint of gleam in her eye. Sure enough, soon after she left, I heard the rattle of dishes in the kitchen. I think she's slowly recovering, taking an interest in life again.

Praise the Lord! ✖

*March 2*

Grandpa Dave's drove over tonight to see the baby. They had an extra horse tied on behind their buggy, and he wants Nate to try it. He claims that it is a good one, so hopefully that will be the end of our horse troubles.

When Annie saw little Crist, she threw back her head, laughed heartily, and remarked, "Why, he doesn't look like a baby. He looks like a wise little man!"

At first I felt a bit peeved, but anyhow, she probably meant Crist was "wizened," wrinkled as he is. Yet Crist does have a wise, alert look on his face!

Nate has a backache and spent most of the day lying around. I guess it's good that Barbianne likes to work outside and do chores. But still, much of the time, the kitchen looks a mess, and I fear for what visitors will think.

Thus I was so glad to see Grandma Annie walk in. She rolled up her sleeves and got to work right away. Priscilla was up most of the forenoon and was a big help in entertaining the children and keeping them happy. She showed them picture books and told them stories.

When Priscilla went back to her bed, they came and crowded around my bed, trying to climb up, and wanting to hold little Crist. It was rather a relief when Barbianne came in and took them out to the kitchen.

Poor little tykes! They're all still just babies themselves, needing to have their share of being held and cuddled, too. ✄

*March 11*

*B*etween Nate's back trouble, little Crist's bellyache spells, and the demands of the other children, I'm beginning to feel like I'm being pulled in a thousand directions. What happened to all my resolutions to be sweet and kind, to never raise my voice, to only speak gentle words and have smiling eyes, to never give hasty, sharp replies?

It almost seems as though weariness, confusion, and noise have obscured my vision of "life's fleeting joys," as it says in that little poem.

Nate's back has gotten a lot worse, instead of better, and he stays in bed all the time now, lying as still as possible because of the pain.

We've had Dr. Wing out, and he gave Nate some pain-killers, but aside from that, there's nothing to do but rest it out. It's something he's had trouble with before, and it seems to get worse during times of stress, Dr. Wing said.

When he said that, I thought to myself, half bitterly, *So, now he has me for a wife, and five small children so close together. I guess it's too much stress for Nate at his age!*

This forenoon he called to me from the bedroom in an irritable voice, "Can't you just keep the children quiet for at least fifteen minutes?"

I thought, *Oh sure, Hubby! I'll just tape their mouths shut with Scotch Tape, and whip them all soundly and send them to bed, like the old woman who lived in a shoe and had so many children she didn't know what to do.*

I was so tired, myself, feeling weepy and tearful. Ideas whirled through my mind: Nate was a peaceful old bachelor until I barged into the picture and spoiled everything for him. He's too old to stand the noise of a colicky baby and four other preschoolers.

I bundled up the four oldest ones and sent them out with Barbianne. Then I took Baby Crist into the sitting room to Priscilla's bed and asked if she would tend him for awhile. That freed me to join Nate in the bedroom.

"Do you have to spend all your time with your precious children?" he asked in an accusing voice. "Don't you have any time for me when I'm having so much pain?"

Suddenly I felt ashamed of my thoughts. Poor Nate! I hadn't been thinking about what he was going through at all, only how tired and worn-out I myself was.

"I'm sorry," I told him. "Do you want me to massage your shoulder blades?"

I knew I couldn't touch the lower back, where the pain is, but rubbing the upper back seems to relieve tension.

He nodded, and as I gently massaged, I felt him relax. Soon his deep breathing told me he was drifting off to sleep.

"I mustn't blame myself," I decided. Nate is the kindest of husbands when he's feeling well, and when he's not, he would try the patience of a saint. Maybe if I take time for a nap, I'll become a little sweeter myself. ✖

*March 15*

*L*ittle Crist is a full-fledged colicky baby. Sometimes I pace the floor with him until I'm absolutely exhausted, wondering why I ever thought it would be fun to be a mother. When I get impatient with Crist, I feel like a failure as a mother. Then seeing the housework piling up and not getting it done makes me feel worse.

Two days ago I told Nate we'll simply have to get a *Gnecht* (hired man), for I must have Barbianne's help in the house. Nate's condition has improved somewhat, but he's still not able to work. At least he doesn't have so much pain anymore. Priscilla is usually up part of the day but is still too weak to do much.

We were able to get eighteen-year-old Rudy Yoder at short notice. This is nothing short of a miracle, an answer to prayer. Grandpa Dave somehow managed to recruit him for us.

Rudy's other plans had changed at the last minute, and so he's scheduled to be here tomorrow morning. He'll be able to go ahead with spring plowing and other farmwork. I had thought we'd have to be satisfied with a fourteen-year-old at such short notice, but this is much better.

We've been having plenty of visitors, both to see the baby and to visit Nate, and to encourage Priscilla, too. Everybody seems to have some suggestion or advice for both the colic and the backache, some sure cure or old home remedy.

One old grandmother even suggested that the baby may be liver-growed (whatever that is). To cure him we should pass him three times backward around the leg of the kitchen table, or something like that.

I started to laugh helplessly—I just couldn't help it! I know she was insulted, for she was in earnest about it. Some of the visitors really do have good advice, but it's hard to know which to take and which to leave.

It's discouraging to get up in the morning and see the supper dishes still in the sink, the laundry piled high, and crumbs on the floor. Because of a colicky baby, I'm not able to give the other children their share of care.

I'm just hoping that Barbianne will buckle herself down to housework now that Rudy will be here. If she does, things are bound to get better around here soon.

We're also feeling a lot better since we found out we

won't have to hand over the $7,000 that truck driver requested after he hit our horse on the road. If any money will be collected, it will be done by the insurance company, not the driver.

These past few days I've been feeling out of tune with God, so busy that I didn't take my daily quiet time of Bible reading and prayer.

O God, forgive me, help me to get out of my rut and back into sweet fellowship and dependence upon you. No wonder my days are chaotic. ✖

*March 19*

*R*obins are singing joyously once again! What a good example they are for us humans. Lately I've felt as though an element of joy had dried up in my heart. Going for a walk in the fresh air today helped me get things back into their proper perspective. It was like looking at my life from another angle, from a distance.

When I headed back and saw our house nestled there among the trees, the house where we live and love and cry and work and feel frustrated and hope and rejoice together, I thought, *All this shall pass away.*

Sometime when I'm old and perhaps alone, I'll think back to now with homesickness and longing. So I resolved, in the midst of our petty trials, to keep joy alive and to bring laughter into each day.

Rudy already seems like a part of our family. There's never a dull moment when he's around. He and Barbianne hit it off well, almost too well, in fact. They seem to communicate with each other without the rest of us knowing what they're talking about. They're constantly teasing each other at the table, with their quips and jests, and sometimes only with their eyes.

Rudy knows how to make people laugh, and he's generous with his compliments. Barbianne knows she has to help more in the house now, but she'd much rather be out with Rudy. This morning she washed the dishes in five minutes flat, swished the dishrag over the table, brushed up a few crumbs under the table, and then she was off, without even consulting me.

Ten minutes later I heard the clatter of wheels. Looking out, I saw her and Rudy on the big flat wagon with the two workhorses hitched, bouncing through the barnyard at a fast clip, probably going stone picking. She was driving, and the wind was blowing her covering straight out in back. Only the pins were keeping it from blowing away entirely!

Barbianne is spunky and fun-loving, always laughing and carefree, but I'm thinking she should still be under a mother's supervision. Already I'm wondering if there's something brewing between Barbianne and Rudy. Of course, they knew each other well before coming here, but now they're together so much, and neither of them is going steady. ✖

*March 20*

*P*riscilla is up and around more and more these last few days. She's had some blood work again, and her levels are much improved. Tonight while she and I were alone in the kitchen, she seemed to want to talk about herself and Henry.

"You know," she said contemplatively, pushing a few stray curls under her covering, "I think it's good that Henry left, that he and I didn't get married."

"Why so?" I wanted to know. "What if Henry learned that his wife had died and came back and wanted to marry you. Wouldn't you say yes?"

She shook her head. "I honestly thought I was completely healed and that my blood disorder problems would never come back. Now I know that isn't so. It could come back at any time. That wouldn't have been fair to Henry. No man wants an invalid for a wife.

"For a while there, I had a hard time forgiving Henry," she went on. "Why didn't he at least say good-bye properly? Why didn't he talk things over with me before he left? And I thought he must've lied to me, because on our first real date, he told me he wasn't married. But I suppose he meant that he wasn't married anymore.

"He probably figured it would be easier on us both if he just up and left. At any rate, I've freely forgiven him, and I pray for him every day, wherever he is, that God will hold him in his care and keep his protecting hand over him." She brushed away a few tears. "I'll never quit loving him."

My heart ached for her. She still cares—cares deeply, but she's bravely carrying her cross with a smile. Selfishly, I had been preoccupied with my own little cares and worries, forgetting that others have a much heavier load to bear.

O God, forgive me, and help me to be more sensitive to others' needs. "Let us pray for each other, not faint by the way, / In this sad world of sorrow and care; / For that home is so bright, and is almost in sight, / and I trust in my heart you'll go there" (A. S. Kieffer). ✖

*I* had a letter from Dottie Rogers on Monday. She kept exclaiming over and over about how I'm caring for two babies, wondering how I manage. Dottie claims she'd never be able to care for a second one so soon. She thinks it will be at least five years before she's ready for another baby.

Sometimes I wonder, too, how I'll manage. So many nights I walk the floor in the kitchen with little Crist, keeping the door to the bedroom closed so Nate won't be disturbed by his crying. As I walk, I try to count my blessings.

I'm glad Nate's pain is not so intense anymore. I'm glad Priscilla is recovering. I'm glad Amanda is doing so well and that her glutaric acid levels haven't gone up. I'm glad little Crist is healthy, and that this colic is something he will outgrow.

Last night I was walking with Crist in the dark kitchen until he fell asleep. When I was about ready to tiptoe into the bedroom with him, I heard a thump right outside the kitchen door in the washhouse. I froze, listening carefully, my heart thumping with fear.

There it was again, stealthy noises, a scraping sound, and another thump. Quickly I laid the baby in his crib and was about to wake Nate. Then I remembered that he wouldn't be able to investigate anyway. Without thinking what I was doing, I grabbed the flashlight on the bureau, ran noiselessly into the kitchen, and yanked open the door to the washhouse.

At the same time, someone was running out through the outside door of the washhouse. All I saw was a man's shoe disappearing around the corner. Frightened speechless, I ran back into the kitchen. Through the window, in the moonlight, I saw him running, carrying a large wheel or some large contraption.

"Nate!" I called urgently. "*Dabber kumm!* (come quick). The thieves were in the washhouse!"

The stair door opened, and Rudy burst into the kitchen. "Quick, give me the flashlight!" he shouted. "I saw a man running toward the barn."

In a flash he was out the door, and I heard him yelling, "Hey, stop thief!"

There were more shouts, then the roar of a pickup starting up. A few minutes later, Rudy came back, carrying the same contraption.

"It's Great-Grandma's spinning wheel," Nate gasped.

Rudy carefully set the spinning wheel down in the middle of the kitchen.

"Now who would've known that it was stored in the washhouse attic, and that it's a valuable antique?" Nate was really astounded. "Could you make out who it was?"

"No, unfortunately, I couldn't," Rudy lamented. "He was too far ahead of me. At least I scared him enough that he dropped the spinning wheel."

It makes me jittery to think about it. The thieves are getting bolder than ever, coming into the house like that. Well, not exactly the house, maybe, but the washhouse is attached to the house.

It's getting to be nerve-racking, and I wish we could catch them. I have a strong suspicion that the guys in the trailer are the guilty ones, and that Rusty never killed their rabbits. They just wanted him dead so they could steal here again. But I have no way to prove it. ✖

*N*ate's back is finally well enough for him to ride in the carriage again. So this afternoon he asked if I wanted to go along to try out the new horse. Rudy had driven him a couple times and said he's decent and has speed, but doesn't hold hard (try to run away with the rig), so I jumped at the chance to go along.

It seemed so long since I've been away, and I felt almost as free as a bird. Nate seemed like his old happy self again, and it was a lovely spring day. The willows are greening, spring flowers blooming, and birds joyously singing praises to their Maker.

"How would you like it if I'd buy the Foster farm that's coming up for sale next fall?" Nate asked, half shyly. "For years already I've been thinking of buying that farm when it becomes available, because it's joined to our farm on the south side. I've been undecided though, these last few weeks, but now I've made up my mind. If you're agreed, I'd like to buy it."

"The Foster farm!" I gasped. "But that's ninety acres of prime limestone soil, and the buildings are in good condition and all fixed up for dairying. Don't you realize what a huge price that will bring?"

Nate nodded. "Yes, but Grandpa Dave told me he'll put some money in, so I won't have to go to the bank. I've been dreaming of this for so long, and I'd like to try it."

"Would we have to move then?" I was almost holding my breath while I waited for the answer.

"We could decide that later. Say, look at this horse's nice trot!" Nate exclaimed. "This is a real horse, I'd say. He doesn't shy off, either."

I had been so absorbed in talking about the farm that I never even thought about the horse.

"We could call him 'Speedy,' " I suggested. "He's fast and he hasn't once tried to slow down to a walk."

"Which is a good thing for a woman who hasn't got any patience to spare," Nate teased. "At least you won't be throwing rocks at this one!"

We laughed, and it felt so good to have Nate back to his usual good-natured self.

"There, you can see the buildings." Nate enthusiastically pointed across the field to the Foster farm. He turned the horse in at the lane, and we circled the barn.

"Yes sir, everything's in good shape, ready to go." He seemed almost boyish in his enthusiasm, whistling a happy tune.

"There will probably be a few developers at the sale," I reminded him. "They can outbid the farmers any day."

"Nope!" Nate said cheerfully. "This land's zoned for agriculture only. I'll bid until I have it." He winked at me, then grinned.

I don't know—he sounds mighty overconfident to me, but it's so nice to see him in high spirits once again. Our little jaunt did me good, too, and I felt refreshed and ready to "take up the battle" again with my colicky little elf man. ✄

*April 5*

On Wednesday a blue car drove in the lane, and a sad-looking man came to the door, asking to see Nate, or rather, the man of the house.

"I've had a series of misfortunes," he said wearily. "First I lost my job, now my wife's in the hospital, and our baby's only six weeks old. We have five other children as well. Also, my dad lives with us, and he constantly needs expensive medicine.

"On top of all this, the landlord is threatening to throw us out if I don't have the rent by tonight. I'm $50 short and wondering if you could please spare me that much."

He looked pleadingly at Nate, and I felt my heart going out to the poor man. I could imagine those little children and a tiny baby and a feeble old man, huddled out in the streets, homeless and hungry, the children crying for their mother.

I hoped Nate would help him. Didn't Jesus say, "I was hungry and you gave me no meat," and "If you have helped one of the least of these my brothers and sisters, you have done it unto me"?

Yet I needn't have worried. Kind-hearted Nate got out his wallet and handed the man $50.

The stranger took out his handkerchief and wiped his eyes, saying, "Oh thank you, thank you," in a broken voice. "You can't imagine what this means to me! If I ever get back on my feet, I'll pay you back, that I will."

He was all smiles when he left, and it gave me a good feeling to know that we had helped him.

That evening Grandpa Daves came for a visit and said the same man in the same blue car had also stopped at their place and at more of the neighbors, asking for money, but he told them an entirely different story. There he said his son had been in a bad accident, and his wife had left him with five small children to care for, and that he needed money for groceries.

They also gave him money, and then later in the day, Emanuel Yoder saw him staggering out of the *Wattshaus* (saloon), very drunk. What an awful feeling to know that we helped him to that!

Next time someone comes begging, we won't give money at all. We'll offer things like potatoes, turnips, and other vegetables. If they refuse them, we'll know that they aren't really in need. ✖

*April 8*

*W*e had a letter from Isaac and Rosemary today. This time Isaac wrote, too. They still like it a lot in Minnesota and urged us to visit them sometime. But the real reason they wrote has me quite excited. *Henry Crawford* has been boarding with them all winter!

Henry had asked them to keep his presence there a secret from us and Priscilla. But now they wonder if we know of any reason why he couldn't partake of communion with their Minnesota congregation. Henry has been faithfully attending church all winter and has a job going out with a carpenter crew there.

Nate talked with the ministers tonight, and they feel that Isaac should try to find out a little more about his being separated from his wife, and whether a reconciliation wouldn't be possible. Of course, if it's true that she has married someone else, then that's out.

Nate is sitting at the kitchen table now, with pen in hand, laboriously writing a letter to Isaac. He says it goes hard for him. He hasn't written a letter for over twenty years!

I'm holding Crist as I write this. His little eyelids are fluttering open and shut as if he's trying to fight sleep. Dear, sweet little innocent baby! What does life hold for you, my precious little son?

Sometimes I feel almost guilty for having brought such sweet, innocent souls into this world of sin. But on the other hand, I've taken part in giving them the wonderful gift of life, sharing with them experiences of God's love, his provision of salvation, a precious heritage, and the beauties of God's handiwork in nature.

Before me, in a little glass vase, is a bouquet of lovely, fragrant pink, white, and purple hyacinths and bright yellow daffodils. To me, they're a symbol of God's love, goodness, and mercy. Jesus says, "Suffer little children to come to me, and forbid them not."

Dear God, help us to lead them to you, give us wisdom for nurturing and disciplining, for training them up in the way which they should go.

Dora is so beautiful: help her also to have an inner beauty of Christlikeness. Peter is so strong, a husky chap: help us to direct his energies into the proper channels, to live for you and serve you.

Amanda's health is not the best: yet help her to be spiritually healthy and strong. Little Sadie, with her dark curls and bright eyes: lead her in the paths of righteousness, and elfin Baby Crist, too.

Keep their footsteps from straying, and draw them heavenward. O Lord, undertake for me. I am such a weak and imperfect parent. ✖

*G*loria Graham was here to-night with her precious Kitty Kat. Her pet is looking as gorgeous and pompous as ever, still bedecked with pink ribbons, and purring contentedly.

Gloria came with a proposal. "Since you took such good care of Kitty Kat last time, and she liked it so much here, would you consider keeping her for a week in May, while I travel again?"

I could hardly believe she had the audacity to ask again, after having threatened to sue last time! To myself I thought, *Lady, I wouldn't consent to take that cat again, not for love nor for money.*

Yet I politely responded, "I'm glad you trust us. But now we have a new baby and more responsibilities, and we can't do it this time."

She pouted a bit, but then became gracious again. In the fall she's moving to an apartment in town. She wonders whether we know of anyone who would want to rent her house.

I told her we'd let her know if we hear of anyone. I heaved a sigh of relief when she left. That cat brings back bad memories!

On Sunday we had welcome visitors, Allen and Polly and the children! So I finally got to see little Daniel! I thought it can't be that I didn't get to see him earlier, but what with Priscilla's troubles, and Nate's bad back, and our balker horse, we just hadn't gotten around to visiting them.

Baby Daniel is chubby, cute, and huggable. He sure takes after Polly. Little Crist looks real scrawny compared to him.

Polly and I had a good old-fashioned, heart-to-heart talk once again. She sure has a way of making a person feel at ease and comfortable. Polly is so jolly and bubbly, I believe she'd be happy in any circumstance. Allen is a lucky man to have found her, and as far as I know, she's still as optimistic as ever.

According to Polly, Mary is a very good *Kindsmaud* (nanny) and never tires of lugging Daniel around. I believe that baby was a gift sent from God in Polly's "old age," almost a miracle like Sarah's son Isaac in the Bible. ✄

*April 17*

*A*nother letter arrived from Isaac—containing almost earth-shattering news, especially for Priscilla. Isaac had questioned Henry and discovered that he has never been married. He lived with a young woman for three years, and they had a baby daughter, but there was no marriage ceremony or vows spoken.

They were living in sin, yes. But according to the rules of the church, if Henry has repented of that sinful relationship and forsaken it, he is free to marry, but only in the Lord.

Isaac wrote that Henry was rather astounded to hear that. He wanted to know, "What's the big difference? Wasn't it a one-flesh relationship, same as marriage?"

It's true—there does seem to be a loophole or inconsistency there. Yet God had never joined them together in a covenant of marriage, so it seems that their union was never sanctioned.

Furthermore, now the woman is married to someone else. So "what God has joined together, let no one put asunder" means to accept *that* marriage.

I ran out to Nate with the letter, breathless with excitement. "Here, read this," I panted. "Henry has never been married after all. Henry is free. He and Priscilla will be allowed to get married."

"Calm down!" Nate exclaimed. "Give me time to read." But when he laid down the letter, he was as excited as I.

"Come to think of it, Henry never did say anything about a *wife* in his letter to Dave and Annie," Nate commented. "He only wrote 'woman.' Why didn't we think of such a possibility before? We should have known—that's the way worldly people do nowadays."

I nodded. "I guess we were too shocked to think that far. And Henry assumed that that was no different from being married, and therefore he wouldn't be able to get married as long as his first partner was living."

"Someone must have said something to that effect, because he had written that he had just found it out the day before," Nate added.

"Shall I go tell Priscilla right away?" I wondered. "I can't wait to see her face light up."

"Might as well," Nate agreed. "Break the news gently," he said with a smile.

If I had expected Priscilla to be wild with joy, I was very disappointed. Her face did light up at first, but then she sobered.

"I can't marry him," she declared sadly. "I still have this blood disorder, and no man wants an invalid for a wife."

*So she had meant it when she said that to me before,* I thought.

"But you're almost well," I protested. "It was probably the shock of Henry's leaving that knocked out your immune system, and your will to live was gone."

Priscilla shook her head. "There will be other shocks in life," she said quietly. "I know marriage to Henry wouldn't be all roses either.

"Would you please write to Isaac? Ask him to tell Henry how I feel about it. It's best that he doesn't come back. I've resigned myself to giving him up, and I don't want to have to go through the battle again."

She kept insisting that I write until I agreed to do so. After all, it's her life. Poor Priscilla! She's sure had some hard knocks in life.

O God, strengthen and comfort her. Help her to make the right decisions. ✄

*April 24*

*N*ate has decided to keep Rudy as hired hand, since he's planning to buy the Foster farm this fall and will need help in farming two farms. His back still isn't strong, and he has to be careful what he does, or the pain returns, so he's glad for Rudy's help.

Priscilla isn't strong enough for heavy work, either, so she opted to do quilting this summer, and Barbianne has been practically begging to stay, too. I know it's because of Rudy. For that reason, I think I should dismiss her, but I don't know if I could manage alone. Baby Crist's colic spells are still as severe as ever, and the thought of all that work piling up reduces me to near panic.

Yet sometimes I can hardly stand to see Rudy and Barbianne act the way they do. Yesterday I watched them planting the garden together, and I think it's Barbianne's fault. She sneaked up behind him, dropped some dirt down inside the back of his shirt, and then ran off giggling.

He ran after her—just what she was asking for—caught her, and stuffed dirt down inside the back of her dress.

I told Nate he's going to have to talk to her and put her in her place. Neither of them are church members yet, and they don't seem to have a serious thought in their heads. ✖

*May 18*

*I* was working in the garden this forenoon, planting tomatoes and eggplants, when I heard a masculine voice behind me, saying, "Hello, Miriam."

I whirled around quickly. There stood Henry, smiling broadly.

"Is Priscilla around here anywhere, by any chance?" he asked.

The door banged, and Priscilla was coming out to meet him.

I must've been surprised speechless, for I hadn't even managed to say hello.

Henry strode quickly toward Priscilla, and for a moment I thought he was going to hug her, but then he quickly dropped his arms at his side.

"Priscilla!" he exclaimed tenderly.

And at the same time she cried, "Henry!" just as tenderly.

They disappeared into the house, and by lunchtime everything was settled. Henry would hear nothing of her excuses that she's not healthy enough to get married. Priscilla's misgivings were swept away by Henry's reassurance.

Grandpa Daves showed up at just the right time, and everyone was talking and laughing at once. At the dinner table, Dave outdid himself in telling amusing stories, but I could tell that Henry and Priscilla weren't listening at all. They were too busy gazing into each other's eyes.

Finally Henry interrupted, "If we all pitch in and help, do you think we could get ready for a wedding here sometime in June?" He turned first to Nate, then to me.

"I think we could," Nate consented. "What do you think, *Frau* (wife)?"

"I guess so, if Rudy and Barbianne are willing to do most of the work," I agreed, smiling.

"That will just be fun, not so, Barbianne?" Rudy said enthusiastically.

"I'll say!" she chimed in. "We'll make them one great, grand wedding."

"Oh, no," Priscilla protested. "We're having a small wedding. None of Henry's relatives will come, and there aren't many on my side. So it's mostly the neighbors and friends in the church district. I'd like to keep it simple."

Henry spoke up. "Do you think anyone would object if we don't have a conventional Amish wedding, and instead of the festivities lasting into the evening, having everyone leave, say at about 4:00 p.m.?"

"I think that should be all right," Dave replied. "Especially if Priscilla thinks it would make her too tired, they'd surely have respect for that."

Nate smiled at me. "Remember our small wedding? And

everyone left as soon as the ceremony was over."

"Aw, that was because you were flat on your back, in bed," Rudy scoffed. "It'll be boring if no one stays for the evening. That's when most of the fun begins."

"If that doesn't suit you young folks, you won't be invited," Priscilla teased.

"Then we'll come anyway," Barbianne shot back.

"Let them come," Dave laughed. "We'll blacken their faces if they come uninvited. That's an old custom."

I noticed how bright and happy Priscilla looked. Her cheeks were flushed and her eyes sparkled. In preparation for married life, Henry was letting his beard fill out, and now he looked strong and muscular, with a healthy spring tan from working outside.

They sure make a handsome couple. I hope they pick a day near the end of June for the wedding. Soon the peas and strawberries will be ripening, and that will be a busy time. How will we get ready in time? ⌗

*June 24*

What a beautiful day for Henry and Priscilla's wedding! The roses were late this year, and Priscilla filled a vase with them and set them on the sideboard. Their sweet fragrance perfumed the whole room.

I thought of the song "I am going to a city, where the roses never fade. / Here they bloom but for a season, and their beauty's soon decayed."

Yes, we did get ready in time. Now it's evening. The guests left early at Priscilla's request. It was a lovely, orderly wedding, and even Rudy and Barbianne behaved well.

We all could sense that it was a holy and sacred time when the bishop arose and instructed Henry and Priscilla to give each other their right hands. He clasped his hand over theirs, then asked: "Do you believe that matrimony is an ordinance instituted of God, and confirmed and sanctioned by Jesus Christ, and that you must therefore enter upon it in the fear of God?"

Henry's yes was clear and firm, but Priscilla's voice trembled, and I noticed her covering string quivering at the side of her neck.

Each was then asked a few more questions. "Henry, are you willing to love and cherish Priscilla, provide and care for her in health and sickness, in prosperity and adversity, exercise patience, kindness, and forbearance, live with her in peace as becomes a Christian husband . . . ?"

Priscilla was questioned similarly. When both had answered yes to the questions, the bishop pronounced the blessing, saying, "The God of Abraham, the God of Isaac, the God of Jacob be with you and bless this union abundantly through Jesus Christ our Lord, and what God has joined together, let no one put asunder. Go forth as husband and wife, live in peace, fear God, and keep his commandments. Amen."

There were many well-wishers, calling down upon them a lifetime of happiness, *gute Glick* (good luck), and the Lord's blessings.

Maybe life can get back to routine once again, now that the wedding is over.

Henry and Priscilla have rented Gloria Graham's house. She's moving out sooner than she had planned, so they can move in right away. Gloria even offered to have the electricity disconnected so they won't be tempted to use it. I'm so glad they'll be living close by.

Baby Crist is yelling for me, so I must go! ✖

*June 27*

$W$e were busy cleaning up after the wedding today, putting things back in their proper places. While the men were packing benches back into the church wagon, Nate asked Henry about that evening last April. Nate had heard a noise in the barn and found Henry's rig tied to the fence.

Henry searched his mind for awhile and then said, "Oh, yes, now I remember. I had been over at Emanuel Yoder's place that evening, and we got to talking. It got later than I'd figured on staying. When I came by your place, I saw a pickup parked down the road a piece, with its lights off.

"Since I knew you were having trouble with thieves, that made me suspicious. I tied my horse to the fence and went into the barn. Whoever it was ran out the back barn door and fled in the pickup. So I left, too, but I could have kicked myself for not getting their license number before I went into the barn.

"I didn't say anything to you because I figured something had been stolen, and you might blame me."

"So that's why your horse was there," Nate said.

Henry threw back his head and laughed. "If I'd have known you saw my horse tied there, I'd have told you. It sure must have made it look bad for me!"

"Not really," Nate assured him. "Nothing was missing that evening. As time went on, I thought I knew you better than that, anyhow."

Priscilla helped with a right good will, packing away the dishes and putting the house in order. It's amazing how fast she recovered. I wonder whether her illness was partly psychological in origin.

She and Henry plan to go on a trip to Canada to see Niagara Falls and to visit some of the church people around Linwood, Ontario.

They start tomorrow morning by train and will stay a week. I guess it could be called a wedding trip, something unusual for our people. Henry thought it would be odd, not going for a honeymoon, and so they compromised a bit.

It sure is a load off my mind, having that wedding over. Now I can relax and do whatever I want to do for awhile. ✖

*I* just finished cleaning the kitchen, so I'll wait here in the sitting room and write while the floor dries. Barbianne has taken the three oldest along outside, and Sadie is contentedly playing in the toy box. Many times I've been so thankful that she's such a *braaf* (well-behaved) and easygoing child. To have two like Crist, just a year apart in age, would be rather difficult.

Crist's colic is gradually clearing up, and he's gaining better, too. Right now, he's in his infant seat, cooing and gurgling, playing with his toys. I'll be able to enjoy him more now.

Someone has given this definition of a baby: A baby is a small person that makes love stronger, days shorter, nights longer, the bankroll smaller, the home happier, clothes shabbier, the past forgotten, the future worth living for.

How true! ✖

*W*e had a thunderstorm last evening. Now the world is sparkling clean again. The corn is growing so fast, we can almost see it stretch up. The Early Harvest apples are ripe, and we were busy canning applesauce all day.

Barbianne helped well and never once ran off to be with Rudy. She was so quiet, so different from her usual bubbling-over-with-enthusiasm self. More than once I had it on the tip of my tongue to ask what's bothering her. Then I heard her sigh audibly and decided to broach the subject.

"Hasn't life been treating you well lately, Barbianne?" I asked in a lighthearted way. "Or am I maybe just working you too hard?"

"No, it's not that. It's my own fault. I made an awful dumb mistake." She covered her face with her hands, and moaned.

"You're all *schtruwwlich* (uncombed)," Dora told her bluntly. "You should comb your hair."

Barbianne laughed shakily and said, "Little pitchers have big ears."

I suggested to Dora, "Would you like to take a snack out to the yard and have a little picnic, all by yourself? With some raisins and cookies, maybe?"

"Yes, yes!" she exclaimed, jumping up and down, and clapping her hands.

"All by myself! The twins and Sadie can't have any 'cause they're still sleeping."

After she had gone, Barbianne confided in me. "It was on Tuesday evening when you had all gone over to visit Priscilla and Henry, and Rudy had gone to see his parents. I was lonely, so I decided to go for a walk.

"I had strolled about a mile out the road when one of those teenage boys that live in that trailer near the woods, came by on his four-wheeler."

She paused to push some *Schtruwwels* (stray hairs) under her covering, then went on. "He stopped, and he looked so friendly. Then he asked me in a nice way if I wanted a ride. I thought, *Well, why not? Here's my chance for a bit of fun.*

"He told me to hop on back, and I did. And, Oh! I was never so frightened in all my life. We went around corners on two wheels! And the awful things he said! It was terrible. He said he was going to kidnap me and things like that.

"He took me into town, and once there, he turned around and headed back. When he wanted to turn left to leave the highway, he had to stop for a car, so I jumped off and ran into the field. Oh, it was just awful!" She shuddered involuntarily.

"He came right after me, and I thought he was going to run me down. I ran into the cornfield, and he followed me, first with the four-wheeler, then on foot. I was so winded that I could hardly breathe anymore.

"I came out of the corn at Drafty Dave's buildings, and he came right behind. But when he saw that I was running for the house, he stopped and yelled, 'I'll get you sometime, you blankety-blank girl. You won't get away, I'll get you yet! I mean it.'

"I slipped into the kitchen for safety. Dave's weren't there, but they came home about fifteen minutes later, and I asked them to drive me home. My legs were trembling so bad, I don't think I could have walked. I've been scared ever since, almost too scared to even go outside alone. I can't forget the things he said."

I pitied Barbianne with all my heart, but I couldn't help but think that she had run a risk by accepting that offer for a ride.

"Would you like to go home to your parents until you're over this fright?" I asked. "Maybe you'd feel safer there, farther away from the boys in the trailer."

"No, I'll stay," she quickly replied. "I wouldn't want to tell them what happened. They've scolded me often enough for being too forward. I'm sure I've learned my lesson now."

When I told Nate about it this evening after the others were in bed, he said, "That girl needs to be badly frightened a few times. She's much too bold."

However, he seemed greatly perturbed about the whole thing. He's beginning to feel sure now that those fellows living in the trailer are our thieves. But unless we catch them, there is no way we can prove it. And why just us? Grandpa Daves are also their close neighbors, and Daves have never had any trouble with thieves.

O Lord, help us to know what to do about this, and keep us all from danger, harm, and evil. ✖

*July 20*

    *P*riscilla and Henry had invited us and Grandpa Daves for supper tonight, and we sure had an enjoyable evening. My, it felt good to sit back and not have to worry about cooking. Someone else's cooking always tastes so much better. She had made *Schnitz un Gnepp* (apples and dumplings), and this time Henry took a generous helping. He must be learning to enjoy Pennsylvania Dutch cooking.

The house was spick-and-span, and everything looks so shiny and new. They gave us an interesting account of their trip to Canada. That started Dave off in telling stories about trips he took in his years of globe-trotting.

Priscilla has a stack of pretty quilt tops that she got from the quilt lady, ready to quilt. That's what she plans to do all day while Henry goes out with the carpenter crew.

She asked if she could have Dora for a week to keep her company, and I agreed that it would be no more than fair to let her stay. If Priscilla was willing to give in to Henry on the matter of who gets to raise Dora, she should be allowed to keep her occasionally, too.

Dora wanted to stay, too, and she stood in the yard, waving, as long as we could see her. We came home at 8:30, and at 9:15, as I was preparing the other children for bed, I saw a breathless little figure come "flying" in the lane.

"Dora!" I gasped.

I held open the door, and she ran into my arms, crying, "Mamma!"

After she caught her breath, she said, "I didn't want to stay there after all. I want to sleep in my own little bed."

"Did you run all the way?" I asked.

"No, I got too tired. But then I was afraid of those bad boys in the trailer when I went past, so I ran."

"You poor little girl," I cried. Only four-years-old, and running a mile and a half all alone in the dusk. I gathered her up in my arms again.

"Why didn't you want to stay with Priscilla and Henry? It's nearly dark, and you could've gotten lost."

"I wanted to sleep in my own bed."

A horse and buggy came clattering in the lane at a fast clip, the gravel flying. A moment later Priscilla came running in the door, looking frightened, but her face lit up when she saw Dora.

"Oh, thank God, she's safe!" she said, with a sigh of relief. "We were so worried. Didn't you want to stay with us, Dora?"

"'No, you stay here," Dora murmured.

Priscilla laughed. "Well, well. I guess I'll take baby Crist along, then." She lifted him out of his baby swing and asked, "May I?"

"If you bring him back tonight," Dora stated matter-of-factly.

"I'm sure you would," I added. "He doesn't take a bottle."

"In that case I'd better leave him here. Do you want to go along, Peter?"

Chubby Peter ran to get his strawhat and burbled, "*Ich will mit geb* (I want to go along)." He grasped Priscilla's hand, and waved bye-bye with the other.

"I promise to watch him closely," Priscilla assured me.

As she led him out to the buggy and to Henry, I thought back to the time when Priscilla was an irresponsible young girl, telling me she was never going to have any children. She's come a long way since then.

Tonight Priscilla told me that she and Henry are hoping for a large family of happy, healthy children. And I thought of Psalm 127: "Lo, children are an heritage of the Lord. . . . Happy is the man who has his quiver full of them." ✖

*August 9*

*T*onight Rudy took Barbianne to the young people's singing. She sure spends a lot of time in front of the mirror, preening and primping, getting herself ready. Was I ever that way when I was young?

"*Rumschpringe* (running around) is just great!" she told me. "I love every minute of it. I don't think I'll ever want to get married, because then I couldn't go to the singings anymore."

"That's nonsense," Rudy told her. "That's why girls go to the singings, to try to catch a beau."

Barbianne stuck out her tongue at him and went on puffing up her hair, then pulling it back, to try for the best effect.

"Don't you know it's against the *Ordnung* (church rules) to puff up your hair like that?" Rudy said, with mock severity. "That proves you're getting desperate. Well, don't worry, the boys are falling over each other for you."

Barbianne picked up a hairbrush and ran after Rudy, and he slipped out the door, squawking.

"Why are they acting like that?" Dora asked me on the side. "Why is Barbianne mad at Rudy?"

"They're just having fun," I assured her.

The truth is, they haven't a serious thought in their heads. And they like each other's attentions. ✖

*August 19*

> *D*o all the good you can,
> By all the means you can,
> In all the ways you can,
> In all the places you can,
> At all the times you can,
> To all the people you can,
> As long as ever you can. (John Wesley)

I wish I could think of some way to do good to those fellows living in the trailer, in order to heap "coals of fire" upon their heads. We hardly know them and haven't even learned their names.

Again today we had some more trouble with them, and it could have become serious. Nate and Rudy were making hay when one of the teenagers drove into the field on his four-wheeler and swerved close to the horses, scaring them badly. The team took off at high speed and galloped the length of the field before Nate got them under control again.

The men could have been thrown off and badly hurt. We had a few things missing in the shop again, too. Maybe we shouldn't blame them for that, without any proof, but it does look suspicious. I'm fearing that it will go on until someone gets hurt, or even killed.

I keep reminding myself: "The Lord is my light and my salvation; whom shall I fear? The Lord is the strength of my life; of whom shall I be afraid?" ✖

*September 5*

We all attended the Foster farm sale today. I was hoping Barbianne would babysit for me, but she wanted to go (with Rudy), so I took all the children along. It's not every day that we get the chance to see a farm sold by auction.

Nate was still highly optimistic. I knew he would not easily give up the dream of a lifetime. He was determined not to let the farm slip through his fingers.

A large crowd gathered, and farmers greeted each other with "you got your checkbook along?" or "you got your wife along to sign?" Everyone seemed to be in high spirits and in good-natured, teasing moods.

The auctioneer stepped up to the makeshift podium and called out, "What am I bid for this productive ninety-acre farm, in a high state of cultivation, buildings in excellent shape, located in the heart of Amish country?"

The bidding was lively at first, but then it slowed down as the amount got higher. I nearly sprained my neck, trying to twist around to see who was bidding, but to my disappointment, I saw nothing.

I wondered how the auctioneer knew who was bidding. Probably there was some previous agreement: "as long as I have my arms folded across my chest" or "my hat on at an angle," or something like that. I glanced at Nate and could tell that he wasn't bidding yet.

The auctioneer announced a break then, to give the folks more chance to think it over. Grandpa Dave walked over to Nate and began talking quite forcefully, swinging his fist and smacking it into his other hand.

Soon the bidding was in swing again. I glanced at Nate, and he seemed to be looking right at me. He blinked a quick, barely perceptible wink, and I winked back. A few minutes later he winked again, I winked, too. This happened several more times until I realized he wasn't even winking to me at all; he was only bidding!

I felt so mortified, I wished I could disappear. I just hoped no one saw it. I felt so dumb till I looked around and was relieved to see that no one had even been looking at me.

When the sale was finally over, the auctioneer called out, "Sold to Mr. Nathan Mast."

Suddenly I wished that I had stayed home.

*P*rayer is the burden of a sigh, the falling of a tear; / The upward glancing of the eye, when none but God is near" (Montgomery).

It seems that sighing is all I've been doing lately. What, just *what* is the matter with Nate? He won't talk, he doesn't eat, he lies in bed with his eyes closed, and he won't answer when I ask him what's wrong.

I can't do anything for him. He just says, "Leave me alone, can't you?"

He can't stand the noise of the children. Sometimes he paces the floor like a madman, at other times he's the picture of dejection and misery. It's time to begin thinking of silo filling, but he is not in shape for that.

Grandpa Daves stopped in last evening, and Dave started talking real jubilant and excited. "We did it. We bought the farm!" But when he got absolutely no response from Nate, he was soon ready to leave.

Annie whispered to me, "Is he sick on the deal? Does he wish he hadn't bought it?"

"I don't know," I replied dismally. "He won't talk."

"Well, I'm sure that's what it is," Annie murmured. "It happens every time. Just wait a while, and he'll get over it."

Before Annie went out the door, she turned and said, "Oh, yes, I nearly forgot to tell you: Hannah Raber is visiting in this area. I heard say she's planning to get married to a widower from Ohio, sometime in November, and she decided to visit some friends and relatives around here first."

"Hannah getting married?" I echoed.

"Yes."

I can hardly believe it. She had been engaged to Nate for so long, always putting him off. I felt sure she would never get married. Will wonders never cease!" ✖

*B*arbianne asked for the day off today, to attend "Sister's Day" at her parent's place, and of course I gave her permission to go. It was a busy, hectic day, with Baby Crist being feverish and *gridlich* (fussy) this morning. I got a late start on a huge round of laundry.

When I was hanging out the last load, little Sadie pulled the bag of rolled oats off the counter where it had been sitting since breakfast, and it spilled all over the floor. A hurried glance out the window told me that Rudy was unhitching the horses and would be in for lunch any minute.

So I left the oatmeal lie, grabbed a flashlight, and dashed to the cellar for a can of tomato soup. I slapped together a few sandwiches and plunked the soup plates and spoons on the table in a haphazard way.

I hadn't had time to comb my hair yet, and I looked a sight, with *Schtruwwels* (stray hairs) straggling out from under my covering.

Peter had taken every kettle out of my cupboard and strewn them all over the floor. In the midst of the disarray, Dora cried, "Look Mama, we're getting company! A horse and buggy is driving in the lane."

"What!" I cried. "Oh, no!" I felt my heart sinking as far as it would go.

"It's a woman, and Rudy's bringing her in," Dora announced.

"Quick, Dora!" I groaned desperately. "Help me clean up this oatmeal fast. Grab a broom and the dustpan."

Dora did as she was told, and in her haste the handle of the broom knocked over the pitcher of milk on the table.

"Dora!" I screamed. At that moment the door opened, and in walked Rudy with Hannah Raber. I tried to regain my composure, but I felt almost too flustered. Yet I did manage to shake hands with her, greet her cordially, and invite her to have a seat on the settee.

Too late, I noticed cookie crumbs scattered over the settee cushion. Hannah brushed the crumbs away and gingerly sat down, while I mopped the milk.

"So you have five little children already," she observed, in that prim, mannerly way of hers.

I nodded, not even thinking to explain about Dora. "Have you had lunch already?" I asked. "If not, won't you join us? It's not much of a meal, but it might tide you over until suppertime."

"Why, thank you, I think I'll accept your offer. This afternoon I want to drive over to visit Allen and Polly Keim, and it's quite a drive. I borrowed a horse from brother Elam."

I quickly added more milk to the soup and made a few extra sandwiches. We sat around the table and bowed our heads to say grace.

When everything becomes quiet, that's usually the signal for Baby Crist to wake up and start yelling, and so it was again. I went to the bedroom to get him.

"Nate," I said softly. "Guess who's here? It's Hannah Raber. Don't you want to come out and meet her?"

"No, no!" he said emphatically. "Don't bring her in here, either." He turned his face to the wall.

I sighed as I changed Crist's diaper.

At the table Rudy was entertaining Hannah and trying to help the little ones at the same time. I sat in the kitchen rocker to breast-feed the baby.

"So Nate isn't at home today?" Hannah wondered.

There was a moment of strained silence, then I told her, "Yes, he's home. He's not feeling well and didn't want any lunch."

"Oh" was all she said. I wondered if she was thinking, *Hmmmm. It's no wonder. Such a* schtruwwlich *(un-combed) wife, so many little brats, and such a messy kitch-en.*

After the meal, Hannah washed the dishes and swept up the crumbs and oatmeal. I imagined that she might be remembering that she had had the chance for Nate, and that this could be her kitchen if she had made up her mind sooner. Was she regretting it?

On impulse I asked her, "I've heard say that you're plan-ning to get married in November, or was that a false ru-mor?"

Hannah blushed prettily. "It's supposed to be a secret. I don't know who published us before it was time. But since you've heard about it already, I might as well tell you, it's true. To Owen Coblentz.

"I'll be moving my fabric shop to his place then. He's a widower with two teenaged daughters at home yet, and they'll be helping me in the store."

After the kitchen was tidied and cleaned up, I found I could visit better. I actually enjoyed chatting with Hannah.

When she was ready to leave, Rudy hitched up her horse for her, saw her off, and then came into the house. "Who is Hannah Raber, anyway?" he wondered.

"Oh, just an old flame of Nate's," I said nonchalantly.

"Really? She was quite nice."

Rudy went outside again, but his words had set me to thinking. She *was* quite nice.

I rocked my fussy baby, deep in thought. Was that what was wrong with Nate? Had he met Hannah somewhere? Had he too noticed that she was "quite nice"? Was he wishing that he had married her instead of me? Was that why he was so depressed?

The more I thought about it, the more sure of it I became and the worse I felt. A tear slipped down over my cheek and dropped on top of Baby Crist's tousled head. ✛

*September 15*

*A*t least I'm not experiencing any morning sickness like I did during the last three summers. But I'm feeling tired, and I don't have much enthusiasm for anything. Everything is too much trouble.

Barbianne is back today, and I am so thankful for her help. Rudy opened some corn rows this forenoon, to start the silo filling, so it's that time of year again.

Nate came to the dinner table today but ate only a few bites. He and I remained sitting at the table after Rudy had gone outside and Barbianne had taken the children upstairs for their naps. Now was my chance. I had to ask him.

My words came out in a rush. "Oh, Nate, please tell me, are you wishing you had married Hannah Raber instead of me? Is that why you're so depressed?"

"No, no, a thousand times no!" he cried, banging his fist on the table with such force that Cocky, asleep under the back veranda bench, sprang up in alarm and ran off, whimpering. With not a word more, he got up and went back to the bedroom.

I sighed wearily and muttered to myself, "Methinks thou dost protest too much" (Shakespeare). "That was stupid of me! Of course he wouldn't say so, even if it was so."

Suddenly I wanted to get away. I wouldn't stay here another minute. I couldn't stand it anymore. I'd take my babies and go somewhere else—anywhere. I was sick and tired of seeing Nate so depressed and discouraged.

I ran out and told Rudy to hitch the horse for me. On second thought, I decided to leave the children with Barbianne. I would just go for a drive—drive around the peaceful countryside until I felt better able to cope with my trying circumstances again.

Rudy had hitched the horse and tied him at the gate. I smoothed back my hair and grabbed my bonnet.

It was a gloriously beautiful day, and as I passed the grapevine, the sweet scent of ripening grapes filled my nostrils. Bees were buzzing lazily among the grapes, and a few jays were calling from the trees along the creek. But my heart was dead to the beauties around me.

I untied the horse and climbed in the carriage with the reins. A moment later, a hand took the reins from me, and Nate climbed in.

"Move over," he ordered. "Where do you think you're going, anyway?"

"Oh, Nate!" I cried. "I just have to get away. Everything's getting me down. If only you'd be feeling better."

"Well, if you think this has something to do with what you were asking me about, get those foolish notions out of your head!" he declared emphatically. "I'm in serious trouble, Miriam, and you've got to stand by me and help me."

"What's wrong?" I asked, alarmed.

Nate hung his head, then said quietly, "In all the years I've been farming, I've never once filed income tax returns."

I clutched at his arm. "Nate," I implored. "Tell me it's not true! . . . You'll have to go to jail!"

"Maybe not," he said. "But I'll have to pay some stiff fines and late-payment penalties. I was under deep conviction last spring when I first heard that the Foster farm was to be sold in September. I knew I should pay up, but I desperately wanted to buy that farm. That's what made me so irritable.

"Then I quieted my conscience and made up my mind to go ahead and buy the farm. I resolved not to be torn by indecision. I even used some Scripture to justify myself: 'Happy is the one who condemns not himself in that thing which he allows.' I thought I was able to handle it until I actually bought the farm.

"Now I'm ready to give up my own will. I know I'll lose the farm, maybe even the one we're living on now. But to have a clear conscience and peace with God is worth so much more. Maybe we'll have to live in a little shack in the woods, but if we can still all be together—"

"Oh, Nate," I burst out, "I don't care if we have to live in a shack in the woods, if only you won't have to go to jail!"

We were passing the Foster farm now, and I blurted out, "Oh, dear, what will people say?" It was such a shock to me that I hardly realized what I was saying.

Nate answered matter-of-factly. "I've come to the point where what people will say doesn't matter much anymore.

I've come to the end of myself—lost my last shred of pride. Since I've given myself up, I feel so much better."

"I'm proud of you. But how come you didn't pay income tax? Didn't you know you should have?" I asked, puzzled.

"Well, it was this way: the first few years I was farming, I figured I wasn't liable for any taxes. Times were hard, and I didn't have that much income. Gradually, it got a little better, and I knew I should make reports, but I kept pushing it off.

"Property taxes were high. When I paid them, I reasoned that anyhow, I wasn't benefiting from the things taxes were funding, such as military upkeep, schools, and road maintenance. We don't believe in war, I didn't have children in school, and I didn't use the roads much at all.

"The longer I kept putting it off, the harder it got, until it came to this. I can't believe how much better I feel since I made the decision. Since I bought the farm, I've felt like a hypocrite, double-faced, untrustworthy, a lawbreaker."

"I'm proud of you for making that decision," I affirmed. "He who confesses and forsakes sin finds mercy."

✖ ✖ ✖

Only a few more pages, then this journal, too, is filled. This really has been a winding path, filled with joys and sorrows, tears and laughter, hopes and discouragements, sunshine and shadows.

It was a severe blow to my pride to find out that we were not even law-abiding. While we were trying to point others to "the way, the truth, and the life," we weren't living right ourselves.

Never once did I think about filing income tax returns.

That first spring with Nate, my mind was preoccupied with having twins, and also having a baby the next year and the next. I was depending on him to take care of all the financial matters.

It was a real disaster for me to find it out about the tax liability. So often when calamities fall on us, we are apt to think like both Isaac and Priscilla did: Is God angry with me, or has he forsaken me? Doesn't he want me as his child anymore?

I pictured us living in a little shack in the woods, cast out of the church, hated and despised by all, and forsaken by God.

In the past, when I heard that misfortune struck for other people, I thought, *Surely God's grace is sufficient for them.* We know that the Lord even told the apostle Paul, "My grace is sufficient for you, for my strength is made perfect in weakness."

Paul then declared, "Most gladly therefore will I rather glory in my infirmities, that the power of Christ may rest upon me."

I think the German translation makes it a little plainer: *Lass dir an meiner Gnade genügen; denn meine Kraft ist in den Schwachen mächtig.* That sounds as though we have to bow down and partake of the Lord's grace by faith. Like the little verse: "Prayer is a river at whose brink / Some die of thirst while others kneel and drink."

If we believe that God is chastening us to draw us closer to him, and if we kneel and by faith partake of his grace, it will be sufficient for us.

Yet I'm wondering what the future holds for us. Will Nate have to make a confession in church? Will we be excommunicated and put in the ban?

I expect that since Nate is taking the initiative to pay all the taxes he owes, instead of someone else reporting him, the penalty won't be as severe. Anyhow, I'm hoping for that. I don't see how I could bear having Nate go to jail.

I'm also counting on getting a new journal soon. It helps me to write down my thoughts and feelings and prayers. I'd like to give the new journal a pleasant, cheerful title, but maybe it will have to be something like "A Journey into Humiliation" or "A Little Shack in the Woods."

I'm wondering if we'll ever be able to prove who our thieves are and what their motive really is. I hope it will be soon.

Nate has apologized for treating me shabbily. It's so good to see him happy, loving, and kindhearted again. He's playing with the children and doing small favors for me—helping to make our home a place of love, laughter, and happiness—like the nest I had dreamed about so long ago.

Sometimes I wonder how Nate can be so optimistic. I guess it's because he has fought his battle and won—and I am still in the midst of my struggles to accept it. I'm staking my hope on the promise that the Lord's grace is sufficient for me, if I humbly do my part.

I am clinging to Psalm 23 to help get me through the shadows:

The Lord is my shepherd, I shall not want.
He makes me lie down in green pastures.
He leads me beside still waters.
He restores my soul:
He leads me in the paths of righteousness
for his name's sake.

Yea, though I walk through the valley
of the shadow of death,
I will fear no evil: for you are with me.
Your rod and your staff, they comfort me.
You prepare a table before me
in the presence of my enemies.
You anoint my head with oil; my cup runs over.
Surely goodness and mercy shall follow me
all the days of my life,
and I will dwell in the house of the Lord forever.

(Psalm 23) ✖

# Scripture References

**YEAR FIVE**
*Oct. 16:* Rom. 8:28 (further allusions here and there).
*Nov. 21:* Ps. 116:15.
*Dec. 25:* 2 Cor. 9:15; 1 Pet. 5:7.
*Dec. 29:* Mark 16:15.

**YEAR SIX**
*Jan. 25:* Matt. 14:31; 1 Pet. 5:7.
*Feb. 5:* 1 Thess. 5:17.
*Feb. 28:* Isa. 41:10; comments adapted from *Spirit Fruit,* by John M.
Drescher (Herald Press, 1974).
*Mar. 10:* Eph. 4:32; 1 Cor. 13:12.
*Mar. 23:* Prov. 3:6.
*Mar. 28:* Matt. 28:20.
*Apr. 7:* Eph. 5:16.
*Apr. 15:* Phil. 4:7.
*Apr. 30:* 2 Cor. 12:9.
*May 11:* Isa. 53:6; John 15:5; Luke 9:23; 14:27; Matt. 11:28; 2 Pet. 3:9;
John 6:37.
*May 17:* Prov. 28:10.
*July 29:* John 19:30.
*Oct. 23:* Ps. 23:6.

**YEAR SEVEN**
*Apr. 5:* Matt. 25:35-40.
*Apr. 8:* Matt. 19:14.
*Apr. 10:* Gen. 17—21.
*Apr. 17:* Mark 10:8-9.
*July 20:* Ps. 127:3, 5.
*Aug. 19:* Rom. 12:20; Ps. 27:1.
*Sept. 15:* Rom. 14:22; Prov. 28:13; 2 Cor. 12:9; John 14:6; Ps. 23.

## The Author

The author's pen name is Carrie Bender. She is a member of an old order group. With her husband and children, she lives among the Amish in Lancaster County, Pennsylvania.